MW01140957

To My FRIENDS BRUCE & LINDA.
BEST WISHES!

Murray R. Weph...

Secrets of a Soldier

MURRAY DOPKING

FriesenPress

Suite 300 - 990 Fort St
Victoria, BC, V8V 3K2
Canada

www.friesenpress.com

ISBN
978-1-5255-0365-8 (Hardcover)
978-1-5255-0366-5 (Paperback)
978-1-5255-0367-2 (eBook)

1. FICTION, WAR & MILITARY

Distributed to the trade by The Ingram Book Company

Forward

I wish to dedicate this book to the memory of the 31 Battalion of the Canadian Expeditionary Forces (CEF) as well as all soldiers of the Great War on both sides of the conflict. This war was presented with the ill-conceived notion that it would end all wars. Alas, the world has been involved in global conflict since 1914. In a war, there really are no winners. We all end up losing.

Thanks

My sincere thanks to my family for their support and encouragement while I've immersed myself in this, my first novel. Greatly appreciated.

I love you all!

Chapter One

I WAS JUST PUTTING the breakfast dishes away as the telephone rang. Grabbing a towel to dry my hands, I picked it up on the third ring.

"Hello?" I said.

The voice on the other end said, "Patty, is that you?"

"Yes, Mom, who else would it be?"

"How are you doing, dear?"

"Fine, Mother. I thought you were getting your hair done this morning. Is everything okay?"

The line went silent for a while, and then my mother said, hesitatingly, "Patty, I have to talk to you; it's quite important! Can we meet for coffee this morning? Please?"

"Mom, what is it? Are you sick?"

"No, dear, not really, but I haven't slept much all night. There's something on my mind and, well, we need to talk."

"Mom, what's wrong? You're starting to scare me."

"Patty, how about that café in the mall—Albert's, I think it's called. Is that okay?"

"Yes. Yes, of course," I replied. "Are you sure you are alright?"

"Don't worry, Patty. I'll meet you there in an hour. Goodbye, dear."

And just like that, she hung up...again. My mother has been doing this to me all my life. She doesn't explain things, just stops a conversation in the middle and hangs up. She drives me crazy!

Dozens of scenarios started playing out in my mind. Mom's got cancer. Her heart's acting up again. Someone's died or is about to...why does she always do this to me?

Everything they say about mothers and daughters is true. Why couldn't I have had sisters instead of two brothers? Then we could have shared all the drama. My brothers never have to get involved; it's not fair! I've got forty-five minutes to get there.

"Hi, Patty! How are you?" Rose was always so pleasant and easy-going. A perfect hostess for the coffee shop. "Your mom's in a booth by the window in the back."

"Thanks, Rose, I see her waving." Making my way down the aisle, I slid into the booth across from her. I could see she was upset. "Mother, what's this all about?" I asked.

Wringing her hands and not wanting to look me in the eyes, she said slowly, "It's about your father."

Now I was sure she had lost it. "Dad? Dad's been dead for years!" I said incredulously.

"Patty, why is Ross sending for your father's war records? Did you put him up to this?"

"Mother, what are you talking about?"

"You told me yesterday that Ross was sending away for copies of his grandfather's war records."

"Yes," I replied, "he wants to research Dad's time in the army. You know, he never talked much about it, and Ross is just naturally interested in what Dad went through in World War One. He's the oldest grandson, and the government is allowing access to those old files now."

"Why couldn't he just leave things alone?" She looked straight at me, her eyes filling with tears. "Oh, Patty, I'm so sorry!"

Chapter Two

How the hell did this happen? Eighteen months have passed since we left Calgary. The 31st Battalion had been able to muster over 1200 men, farm boys and clerks mostly. Young men full of ideals and propaganda, fed to them by the desk-pounding politicians and clergy of the day.

Six weeks of training and we were ready. "Yeah, we're going to kick Kaiser Bill's ass! This war will be over in six months, a year tops, no problem!" What a load of crap!

A sniper's bullet ricocheted off something a yard away from me. That one might have had my name on it!

"Stupid bugger! Snap out of it!"

"Hey, old man." That's what this new replacement had decided he was going to call me. Twenty-five years old and living in these shithole trenches. I guess I probably looked the part. "Any tips for staying alive?" he asked.

"Yeah," I slowly replied, "When that whistle blows, crawl—don't stand up—and fall into the first shell hole big enough to hide your sorry ass! And don't ever call me 'old man' again, or you'll taste the working end of my bayonet!"

"Sorry, mister! I didn't mean anything by it!"

As I looked into the fresh-faced kid's eyes (this one couldn't even manage chin stubble), I replied, "It's okay. Got your gas mask ready?" I noticed he had pissed himself.

Just then the whistle blew, and over the ridge we went. Stupid bastards! Every one of us. The smell of gunpowder, mustard gas, and blood was everywhere.

I made it through another charge and found a large crater to hide in. The deafening din of bullets and shrapnel screamed overhead. Through the opaque glass of my gas mask, I saw I wasn't alone in my hole...the lifeless eyes of that fresh-faced kid stared back at me. He looked inno-cent, almost cherubic, except the back part of his head was missing.

Another young life snuffed out. Why? For king and country? What bullshit!

Crouched down in that hole and looking over at his face, I knew we just might be sharing this space for a while. With the war screaming on just inches above my head, I was in no hurry to go anywhere. I thought to myself, "Dead people sure don't scare me, and lord knows I've seen enough of them. No, it's the live ones you need to be wary of."

This fellow reminded me of my youngest brother, Joe. I really hoped he was still alive somewhere.

We had left New Brunswick a month after our farm got burnt out. The fire killed Mom and Dad, and left me and my four siblings with lots of bills and no way to pay them. My sister and two other brothers decided to go live with family in Michigan. Joe and me, well, we were going to work our way to Alberta. Lots of opportunity for men not afraid to get their hands dirty! Things were going pretty good for us, too, until this damned war came along...

It was starting to get dark. Soon I could make a move to crawl out. Stuck in "no man's land" is not where I am going to be tonight. Another hour or so. Be patient, Paul, we'll make it. Better start checking everything out: ammo's dry, gun's clean, revolver where I can reach it, knives and short shovel ready, bayonet fixed, limbs all working.

Yep, we're ready to roll! I'm not going to be that easy to kill, Heinie!

The bastard Huns weren't letting up. I wished we had bullets to waste like they do. Finally, the battlefield noise started to lessen; darkness was just about complete. I looked over at the body of my dead companion. "Well, kid, it's time for me to leave you. Sorry you had to die. Maybe I'll see you again on the other side. Wherever that may be. Gotta go!" Quietly, like a rat in the darkness, I scurried over the top of my hole.

The Germans had superior firepower. They had lots of machine guns and repeating rifles. Our Ross rifles were no match for them. Our guns tended to jam up as they got hot. So our rifles were nicknamed the "Canadian Club," as that's all they were good for when they got dirty or well-used. The English-manufactured bullet casings were of soft brass, and caused even more problems. The enemy had ammo to spare, so were able to literally spray an area, whereas we had to make every shot count.

Why do countries decide to declare war on each other and then send their soldiers into battle with inadequate weapons and equipment? Why do young men believe the idiot politicians when they say, "This war will end all wars"? Why do I give a shit?

It started to rain again.

We had become something not quite human. Our instincts were honed razor sharp. It was said that "Bell's Bulldogs" (as the 31st Battalion had become known, named after Lt. Colonel Arthur Bell) were the most efficient killers in the present theatre of war.

Battle-hardened, of necessity. Yes, but much more than that. We were devoid of all normal emotion...except hate. Hate for the Huns, who were trying to kill us, hate for the idiot politicians that got us into this war, and hate for the English aristocracy. They gave military rank to their inbred sons and regarded our colonial lives as expendable. With enough hate working for us, we might even possibly survive this war!

Every one of us knew all too well the account of the Newfoundland Regiment, our brothers in arms, at the battle of Beaumont Hamel. Ninety percent of them were slaughtered in less than an hour. This was a British offensive on the Somme in France. To the English, we were just colonials, a part of the British Dominion, blood less valuable than an English soldier's blood.

Yes, it was the Germans who pumped the bullets into our soldiers, but it was the English who kept ordering them in, wave after wave ordered to move in parade-ground formations in a zigzag path in totally exposed terrain. Most never even made it past the Allied barbed wire. All the while, the Huns were dug in securely and held the high ground on both sides. "Cannon-fodder" was the term used by the newspaper reports.

With the moronic bungling by the British of that battle exposed, it had been decided that our Canadian brass should be in charge of our Canadian military involvement.

October 1916. Word has arrived at the front. The 31st is being rotated back.

Our replacements will be here soon. I wonder how many of our Canadian soldiers are still alive.

Chapter Three

THE MUSIC COMING from the dance hall was loud, boisterous, and happy. I spotted her through the smoky haze as soon as I arrived. She was over along the wall with her girlfriends. She saw me, too, although she quickly looked away. I must say, I cleaned up quite well, with a sharply pressed uniform, neatly trimmed moustache, and combed hair. My frame was almost twice what it was since leaving Canada (everyday war was a workout just to survive).

It felt so good to be clean and above ground!

Her name was Beatrice, Bea for short. She was beautiful. Blonde hair in curls, sparkling eyes, and a curvaceous body that could hardly be restrained by her pretty dress. A smile that could disarm any soldier. I immediately bought all of her dance tickets and set out to win her heart!

"My name is Paul, Paul Bonenfant. I'm from Canada, and I think I'm in love!"

At first, she just looked surprised, and then amused. "Why, you cheeky devil," she replied. "Just because you seem to have a lot of nerve...and the bluest eyes I've ever seen, don't think for a moment I'm going to dance with the likes of you all night!"

"It sounds like you're from Lancashire, and yes, it would truly be an honour to accompany you on the dance floor tonight," I replied, not giving her a chance to say no.

She hesitated and then smiled that beautiful smile. "We'll see," she said. "We'll see." The band began playing a popular song sung by Henry Burr called "Send Me Away with a Smile." For the first time in a long while, life was good again!

Her place (or "flat") was a short distance from the hall. She had told her friends that she was okay and would be walking home with me. I walked as slow as possible, not wanting the night to end quickly. She chattered on about everything and nothing. I tried hard to sound interested. I noticed she never tried to increase our pace either. Was I reading this right?

"Well, this is it," she said, "my door. Surprisingly, I had a very good time. You make me laugh, Paul Bonenfant from Canada. And you dance quite well."

"I had a great partner," I replied. I bent down to kiss her. She didn't pull back. Sweet and gentle at first, then warm and passionate.

"That was nice," she said breathlessly, a faint huskiness now in her voice. "Would you care to come in for some tea?"

"Yes," I replied, "I would like that very much."

The morning sun was working its way through the curtains when her eyes opened. She smiled and asked if I had slept well.

"Like a baby," I said, and smiled back. "How about you?"

With a giggle, she replied, "Very satisfactorily," and then slowly drew back the covers to reveal all those wondrous charms that had given me so much pleasure and comfort all night. "Well?" she said.

What normal man could say no to a beautiful, willing, naked woman? Certainly not this one! The war seemed to be a million miles away...

She managed to arrange some time off from the millinery store where she worked.

I had eight days left before I had to return to my battalion. For now, the war was on hold. We spent our time laughing, loving, and enjoying life. Long walks, short rides in the country, our favourite café. Each of us knew that this might be all we were going to get. In wartime, no one is guaranteed tomorrow. Every moment becomes precious, and even more so for young lovers.

She knew I was leaving soon. "Paul, I'm afraid I will never see you again," she sobbed. This, after another wonderful evening in each other's arms. "I don't want you to go. Please...please don't go back." The tears ran freely down her cheeks now. "Let's run away, hide, and let someone else fight the Germans. I love you! Can't you see that?"

"My darling Bea, I have no choice," I softly explained. "I have to go back. The army won't let me stay just because I met the girl of my dreams. They own me until this war is done. I promise you, I will do everything I can to return to you." In the back of my mind, I knew the odds of me staying alive were not very good.

"Bea, you have rekindled my broken spirit," I said, looking into her sparkling eyes. "I know what it's like to live again. To love and to be loved." I couldn't believe I was putting words to these feelings from my heart! This just wasn't normal for me. Who was this woman, that she put such a spell on me? Other ladies had shared my bed, but it was never like this! What had happened to Paul Bonenfant? Why did I feel like this? "Having you in my arms just feels right. It's where I want to be," I heard myself say.

"Darling Beatrice, you need to know something. The man that you met and loved these last few days also has a dark side. A part that no civilized woman should ever want to involve herself with. This war has made me do some unspeakable things. I have killed...and, to survive, I'm going to have to kill again. Please, please don't get too attached. Let's just be happy we have had this time together."

Looking directly into my eyes now, she stopped crying. Slowly wiping her wet cheeks, she finally spoke. "You big dumbass," she replied, "it's not going to work, you know! I'm so much more than attached! You do what you have to over there. But don't you dare get yourself killed! I'll be here for you as often as you need me. We have something special here, and not even a damned War is going to get in our way! Do you hear me, Paul?"

"Yes, Bea, I do," I quietly replied. I held her close again and could feel the tears on my chest.

Chapter Four

THINGS WERE CHANGING on the Western Front. It seemed like the rest of the world had somehow started taking this war seriously. We were starting to get the latest and best weapons, and replacements were now a regular occurrence, coming in at a steady rate from all parts of the Commonwealth, with Australia really stepping up and supporting the war effort in a big way. Supplies seemed to be coming through at a better rate too.

Both sides were now so very well dug in, though. Both the Allies and Germans had tunnels and ditches running all across Europe. In the infantry, we called our dirt homes "rat cities," as we shared our habitat with the detested vermin. Unfortunately, it was not only bullets causing casualties, but also the tedious days, weeks, and months of living in those damp, filthy ditches. Our boys were suffering from every sort of fungus, pneumonia, lung infections, and myalagia you could imagine. This trench warfare had become an extremely slow but efficient way of killing men in both armies.

It wasn't all hand-to-hand combat. There was one particular humorous incident that still makes me laugh whenever it comes to mind. It had become suspiciously quiet on the front lines. No vicious charges by the Germans or retaliatory returns by us. We had been taking it easy the last few days, looking after letter writing, personal hygiene, cleaning our weapons, and grabbing some much-needed naps.

The trenches were quite narrow, so, to save space, some of us would literally dig ourselves into the sides of the long hole. Everything was fine as long as there was no heavy shelling; then you might find yourself trying to dig out of a tomb.

One of our boys, Jack, had crawled into his cubby hole and fallen asleep. All of a sudden we heard an ear-splitting scream, "Get it off, get it off!" As he rolled onto the main walkway, we saw that he had a rat attached to the end of his nose. The more he tried to pull it off, the more it bit down. One of the nearest soldiers, Scottie, took his rifle and, with the butt-end, smashed the rat into oblivion.

As the rat came loose so did the end of Jack's nose. As you can imagine, there was a lot of hollering, cursing, and a fair amount of blood. Jack began cursing Scottie out, shouting, "What the hell have you done, you crazy loon!"

"You told us, 'Get it off, get it off!' if I remember correctly," Scottie replied.

"Not like that, Scottie!"

"Ah, quit your whining, Jack, it could have been a lot worse!"

"How so, you nutcase?" Jack asked.

Calmly, Scottie replied, "What if you had been taking a leak? You could easily have lost the end of your pecker!"

With that, the entire group of soldiers standing around erupted into uncontrolled laughter. The hapless Jack became just the needed bit of humour we all required. Gallows humour, I think it's called.

There were a great bunch of Canadian men in the 31st battalion, and we Canadians had proven ourselves over and over as a force to be reckoned with. The British were allowing more and more military decisions and strategies to be made by our own Colonel Currie. His ability to organize infantry divisions, quickly mobilize artillery, and coordinate supply lines were having a notable, positive effect. The man was a strategist of the highest calibre.

News had come down to us that our Russian allies were backing off on fighting the Germans on the Eastern Front to focus on a revolution of sorts taking place inside their own country, something to do with a Bolshevik uprising. The scary part was that the Germans would soon be in a position to free up close to a million men to attack us.

As if this war couldn't get more deadly and complicated.

Chapter Five

THE ALLIED FRONT LINES

"Paul, you old dog! I can't believe you're actually standing in front of me!"

"Joey, get your ass over here and give your big brother a hug! I totally lost track of you since Calgary. A few letters made it through, but then they stopped coming. The last was from London...how the hell are you?!"

We slapped each other on the backs. "Sure glad to see Heinie hasn't tagged you yet!" I said.

"It's not for lack of trying, Paul!" Joey said. "If those bastards had been brought up in New Brunswick, they might be dangerous. Do you remember how Dad would get so mad if we had to take two shots to bring down a squirrel?"

"What was it he said?"

"If you don't think you're going to hit what you're aiming at, don't pull the trigger, you dumb buggers!"

"Bullets are expensive!" I chimed in. We both laughed heartily. "Yeah...I often find myself thinking about the old man lately."

"Me too," Joey replied.

"He taught us a lot about survival...and life. *Joie de vivre*, eh?"

"The joy of life," Paul translated. "Seems to have even more meaning lately."

"Still carrying the 'toothpick,' Paul?"

"Saved my life a few times out here; those damn bullets don't always fire properly, but a well-placed blade is always ready."

"Paul, I've never met anyone as good with a knife as you. You're lightning quick, and just as deadly!"

"Unfortunately, I get to practise here a lot," Paul replied.

"From what I hear, you're also very well-respected on the line!"

"Just doing my job, Joey, and trying to stay alive. We've got a good bunch of guys here. We try to look out for each other! So, what's the 151 Battalion doing in our neck of the woods?"

"We're providing protection cover and support for the supply lines," Joey replied.

"The Huns are trying hard to stop as much as they can from getting to you guys here on the front. They've managed to infiltrate and cause us a lot of damage. Under the cover of darkness, small groups of two or three weasel their way in and plant explosives, destroying our bridges, roads, and such. Never taking on any large groups, but generally just being a real pain in our asses! Our biggest fear is the intelligence they may gather as to our troop movements and strengths. Actually, a very sound strategy, if I may say so."

"They're almost as good as we were for stealth back in New Brunswick," Joey continued. "Remember how our Indian cousins taught us how to stalk and hunt at night? Chief Red Dog named you 'Night Puma' because you were able to crawl through the brush and not make a sound. The night sounds never stopped when you were on the prowl."

"Yeah, I remember that," I said. "Kind of a dumb name, but I had to be quiet, 'cause if Red Dog had caught me with his daughter, I would have been history!" We both laughed again.

"Damn! I missed you, big brother! We had some good times! Say, I just had an incredible idea, as long as you're willing to hear me out?"

"Why not, Joe? Let's get off to the side and have a listen to your proposal."

"Is what you are saying even possible?"

Incredulously, my sibling was talking about things that the ordinary soldier didn't even know existed.

"Just say yes, Paul... I'll look after the rest," he assured me.

"Yes, it is Joe. Make it happen, that is if you're not insane or crazy." I grinned back at him.

"By the way, this is top secret. You can't breathe a word of what we discussed to anyone. Understood?"

"My word is my bond, Joe. You, better than anyone, should know that."

"Get ready to move out. I'll make the arrangements. You're headed back to England."

"Joey, you seem to have some powerful connections; I'm not going to ask how this happened."

"It's probably best we just leave it alone. I promise, when I can, I'll tell you the whole story, Paul. For now, we're just two soldiers assigned to a delicate mission. I can say that Canada welcomes your specific qualities and appreciates your skills."

"You are so full of shit, Joey!"

"Be that as it may, I'm glad you got my back, brother!"

"Always will, Joey, always will," I replied.

Incredible as it seemed, here I was back in England, undergoing top-secret training—everything from a crash course in German to something I had never even heard of before, the martial arts. Weapons training of the highest level. Chemical warfare. Intelligence-gathering techniques that seemed to be almost out of a science fiction novel.

My little brother was full of surprises!

We were assigned to small groups or clusters of specialists, usually four to five in a group. Orders came down the chain of command through Joey. He wasn't the head honcho, but was constantly in touch with "Him" or "Them."

Secrecy was of the utmost importance; even our real names were not used. We were told that if we were captured, our existence would be denied. I, like the others selected, were "on loan" to another battalion and our records were adjusted in such a way as to make nothing look out of the ordinary.

I really didn't care; I was still alive, and was able to see Beatrice on a regular basis. *This training can take as long as they want!* I thought.

Life was good again! Playing house with Beatrice seemed like the most natural thing in the world. I loved how she woke up in the morning with her tousled hair all over the place, a smile on her face, and a giggle in her voice. She always had many great notions as to how we were going to spend our day. Lots of those plans included us in various stages of undress and intimate positions that kept me eagerly wanting more.

She was everything a man could want. A cook in the kitchen, a lady in public, and a whore in bed. Maybe "voracious lover" was a better term.

There was no doubt; I was smitten! This girl from Lancashire had my heart. We had been spending every possible moment together, not only enjoying the physical pleasures, but also really getting to know each other. Her mind was quick and sharp.

She was an avid reader and tried hard to keep up with all the things going on in the world—something not common these days with women. She even had the crazy idea that someday women were going to be allowed to vote! I smiled when she told me that and said that it could happen...maybe not in this century...but it could happen.

It turned out her family had ensured that she had gotten a decent education, and they weren't what you would call traditional. She and her two sisters were quite outspoken, with definite opinions on just about everything. I found myself liking that in a woman. Odd how you learn things about yourself...

She was okay with the explanation I gave her of temporarily being reassigned to help train some replacement troops here in England. She knew it was only short-term, but we were happy for whatever time we had.

I felt that I had some pretty big decisions to make. I knew this was something I genuinely wanted for the rest of my life, but the damn war, and all the variables, scared me. The reality was, "How long was I going to be able to survive?"

But then again the idea of not having her in my life, scared me more than facing the Huns in the trenches! I couldn't let her know what I was thinking, at least not yet.

Finally, I was able to introduce Beatrice to Joey, and we managed to spend a couple of social evenings together. One evening, after a fine dinner at her place, when she was in the kitchen, I confided to my brother. "It feels serious, Joe. Tell me, what do you think of her?"

Joey agreed; she was definitely a keeper! After pausing a few moments, he said, "I think you had better not screw this up, Paul! You have someone very special. I envy you; I really wish I had a lady like her in my life. But honestly, Paul, the life we live, as soldiers; it's pretty much day to day. Long-range plans...I don't know, is it wise?"

"Yeah, I know, that's what I'm wrestling with right now, Joe. I appreciate you being straight with me."

From the kitchen came a voice, "Are you two ready for dessert?"

"I hope you baked two pies, because I and this brother of mine both have a real strong Canadian sweet-tooth!

Chapter Six

ADEEP, NUMBING DARKNESS enveloped me. I felt no sensation: no pain, nothing. Slowly, though, a dim light began to penetrate the black. Just a flicker at first, then getting brighter and brighter. I became aware of sound. I thought I was back on the farm, and that the wind was moaning and groaning through the trees.

Nope, that wasn't it! Louder now, voices yelling. Plaintive German cries for help.

Cursing...gunshots...where the hell was I? My eyes were open now, but it was still dark.

Something wet and sticky was running into my face. My helmet was off.

Suddenly all my senses kicked in. There were bodies all around me: mostly dead, others in the process of dying. Both my hands were covered in blood. My gun, out of ammo, lay close by. It was actually steaming in the cool night air.

A gurgling sound to my left startled me. A German soldier was clutching his throat and trying to pull out my "toothpick" from his larynx. His eyes were wide with fear, fully aware of the life exiting his body.

He quit moving, and I quickly pulled my knife out, wiped it on his tunic, and put it back into my ankle sheath. "Sorry, Fritz," I mumbled, "it was either you or me." Grabbing my helmet, complete with a new ventilation hole, and my reloaded gun, I slowly crawled out of the German gunner's nest. The false dawn was starting to show on the horizon, and I needed to get out of here quickly!

I had roughly one hour to make it to the rendezvous point. Daylight was on its way. Our mission was simple: infiltrate under cover of darkness, using stealth and camouflage. Take out specific targets. Gather as much recon intelligence as possible and get back alive.

Because our units officially didn't exist, we wore no Allied uniforms or insignias.

If captured, we were on our own. My men and I were the elite of the Canadian Expeditionary Forces. Identities were nonexistent. We knew each other by code names only. Our motto was "No quarter given, and none expected." There were now over a dozen of us "ghost soldier" groups, usually with anywhere from four to six men in a unit, depending on our specialties. We could effectively blend into any type of terrain and remain hidden until our targets became viable. Our training was ongoing. We were always becoming more skilled and proficient in all our areas of expertise.

Joey had explained to our group, during a training session, that the idea for our existence apparently came from the medieval soldiers known as Templars. They were professional soldiers, knights extraordinaire, experts in the art of warfare. I had never heard of them, but my learned brother seemed to be well-versed. *Full of surprises, that boy,* I thought to myself.

Our commander-in-chief (whom we had never met) was a high-ranking military strategist. He had the full support and backing of the governments of England, France, and Belgium. They wanted this war over with, as soon as possible.

Tonight's raids were the last of a series of territorial probes into German defences. We were now ready to launch the biggest attack on our enemy since the war began. The Allies, and especially the Canadians, were about to rewrite military history! After a thorough debriefing with Joey at a secret field location a few miles back of our front lines, our unit was instructed to return to England.

We had two weeks leave, courtesy of a certain very high-ranking officer.

Joey's parting words to us were, "Well done, men! Enjoy your time off, and get ready to prepare yourselves for the battle from hell!"

As we split up, Joey said he would catch up with me back in England in a few days. I could only wave and acknowledge I had heard him. My focus was that beautiful blonde from Lancashire. All I wanted was to go home to her. Strange, that I equated home with Bea... You know how sometimes out of the blue, a purpose or life decision just hits you? Some might call it an epiphany. Well, in that moment, I knew exactly what I was going to do.

It was a sunny afternoon as I waited outside her flat. The air was crisp and clean. I had just put my cigarette out as

I spotted her down towards the end of the block. Getting up from her door stoop, I raised my arm in greeting. She couldn't see me at first because of the sun shining in her eyes. Then a squeal of recognition and a hearty wave back. I started walking towards her. She fairly flew at me and wrapped her arms around my neck. Light as a feather, I picked her up and spun her around; she laughed and kissed my face.

"Hello, Lancashire!" I said. "Did you miss me?" God, she felt good! I thought to myself, *I was right…yes! This is home!*

Once we were inside, the questions came fast and furious. "How long have you been waiting? Are you okay? When did you get back? How much time off do you have? Are you hungry? I'll make something to eat."

Not saying a word, I just smiled and took a long hard look. She was beautiful.

Stunning, actually, those blonde curls, rosy cheeks, sweet happy voice, and luscious lips.

"Well, say something! You big ox!"

Still speechless, I looked into her eyes, held her face with both of my hands, and slowly and gently said, "I love you, Bea."

The room was suddenly quiet.

"What did you say?" she asked. Tears filled her eyes now, and freely ran down her cheeks.

I replied, "You heard me, Bea; I'm madly in love with you. It sometimes takes me a while to figure things out… but I want you—not just for now, but forever. I've been using this war as an excuse not to commit to anything permanent. What I should have been doing was realizing that love, once you've found it, is the most important thing that exists. No one knows how much time we are allowed, whether a war is raging on or not.

"As someone a lot brighter than I once said, 'It is better to have loved and lost than to have never loved at all.'" With that, I reached into my pocket and brought out a small case with a sparkling diamond ring in it. "Bea, will you do me the honour of becoming my wife?"

The tears still flowing could not cloud the joy and excitement in her eyes. One hand on my arm and the other over her heart, she managed an almost inaudible "Yes..." gasping now, "Yes, Paul. I will...I will!"

Our lovemaking that evening was slowly sensual and deliberate. We took our time: exploring, giving and taking from each other. We both reached a point of exquisite delirium. Gone was the merely carnal lusting. This was different; it was fulfilling and satisfying. I knew once again that this was where I wanted to be. This was home.

The following days were a blur. Our wedding was simple, a rushed assembling of Bea's family and friends. Joey, of course, was my best man. The preacher gave a nice discourse on what the ideal marriage should be: honour, trust, compassion, and love.

Great words and proper goals. But, like Joey said afterwards, "That man has obviously never been to war. Sentiment can only get us killed. Right, big brother?"

I looked at him and slowly said, "No...you're wrong, Joey! This is what a soldier needs: reasons to live and survive!"

"I know what you're saying, Paul, and this beautiful lady has made an impact on how you're thinking. But there's a lot of war left to fight. I need you focused on the task in front of us. Enjoy what's left of your leave. I'm sorry," he said, "but I have to leave in an hour or so. I know...I know...! This is probably the most important day of your life...but you'll understand soon enough why." Joey leaned in closer and spoke so that no one could hear. "We have a very important top-secret meeting scheduled in two days. The entire task force is assembling at 07:00 sharp. You know the location. Like I said before, Paul, she's a keeper. Don't screw this up! Don't worry, I'll be looking out for her when you're not around."

Chapter Seven

THE LARGE HALL was full of an array of the most efficient experts at stealth and killing the Allied Forces had ever assembled. We didn't know each other's identities or origins, only code names. I had served on missions and trained with most of the men.

It was quite a moment. A feeling of proud camaraderie and achievement was prevalent. The idle chatter stopped immediately as the door opened. We all snapped to attention and saluted. Standing there in front of us were Lieutenant General Byng, Major General Arthur Currie, Lieutenant Colonel Andrew McNaughton, and alongside them...Joey.

After returning salutes, Joey spoke first. "At ease, men. Please be seated," he said.

"What we are about to discuss here is TOP SECRET and will NOT leave this room! Major General Currie, the floor is yours."

You could hear a pin drop as General Currie stood and slowly gazed over the room. Finally, in a loud, controlled voice, he spoke. "You men have been instrumental in acquiring intelligence needed to launch this epic military assault on our enemy. What we are about to do will forever change how war as we know it is fought! We and the Germans have almost reached an impossible impasse. Both our lines are so well dug-in and fortified that the cost in lives, to sometimes gain only a few hundred yards, is staggering. THIS CANNOT CONTINUE!

"We have developed a new technique and strategy called the 'creeping barrage.' This procedure will be implemented at a site known as Vimy Ridge. Each one of you men will be trained extensively, then given command ranks of captain to lead existing platoons in the assault on our enemy. Preparations for the movement and placement of artillery have already begun. It will be primarily the job of Canadian divisions to complete this formidable task. We are breaking military protocol in that all of our platoon leaders will have information on all aspects of this operation.

"If certain groups fail in meeting their objectives, then the next in line will carry on. No more confusion on the battlefield! As you may know, Vimy Ridge is high ground, over which the Germans have complete control. They have created deep underground bunkers and fortress cities that are impervious to our biggest guns. All that is about to change!"

Everyone in the audience paid rapt attention to the information being dispensed. General Currie was a mesmerizing speaker. He radiated confidence, and we all looked up to him like the military god that he was. My mind was wandering, though. How in the hell did Joey know these most powerful and influential leaders? He obviously knew each of them on a personal level, too! My younger brother was full of surprises, and I was anxious to ask him a lot of questions.

Our training as platoon leaders began the next day. It felt good to finally have the uniform and rank of an officer. Everyone was eager and upbeat. Another plus for me was that I got to continue seeing Bea. She was my reason to live, and we grew closer by the day.

Chapter Eight

APRIL 5, 1917
VIMY RIDGE, FRANCE

OUR ARTILLERY AND supply lines were now in place. It was probably the best- and worst-kept secret of the war. If the Huns were aware of this massive build-up, they obviously didn't care. After all, in their minds, many had tried to unseat them from their lofty position before and failed. What was a few thousand more dead Englishmen?

I had just finished an in-depth planning session with a group of our platoon leaders, and everything was ready. We had amassed over one hundred thousand men, comprised primarily of the 1st, 2nd, 3rd, and 4th Canadian Divisions, united for the first time against the Kaiser's stronghold.

The adrenalin was pumping. We were now only awaiting orders to begin. As we tried to rest and prepare ourselves for the upcoming battle, care packages and mail from home was being distributed. I opened Bea's letter and slowly read each sentence. My darling wife started out by telling me the latest news in the neighbourhood, and casually mentioned that we would have to start looking for a larger flat. At first, I thought, *What a lot of nonsense, the place we are occupying is plenty large enough for the two of us.*

Then she finally came out and put it in plain English: "WE ARE HAVING A BABY!"

Nothing could have prepared me for news like this! We had never even really talked about having children, what with the war and all. I put the letter down, got up, walked around a bit, then picked it up again and reread it. *This is insane!* I thought. *Incredibly wonderful, but INSANE! I'm about to engage in the biggest battle of the Great War, and my wife decides to have a baby? Is she crazy?!* I wanted to shout, swear, and cry at the same time. Then, what I really wanted, was to just hold Bea in my arms.

"Paul," I told myself, "get it together. Focus on the task at hand (as Joey often said). Don't think! Just get through this and live!" Now more than ever I needed that edge, that killer's instinct. Sentiment would only get me killed!

APRIL 9, 1917
5:28 A.M.

"The week of suffering," the Germans later named it. The heavy barrage of shells raining down on German positions was incredible. Two hundred fifty heavy guns and approximately six hundred lighter-gauge field guns delivered an average of 3500 tonnes of shells daily to the Huns, courtesy of the Canadian and Allied Expeditionary Forces!

It was now time to begin the attack on the ground. "Well, Paul, this is what we have been training for," I told myself. "There's going to be a lot of dying going on today." Hopefully more of them than us. "I'm not that easy to kill, Heinie! Bring it on, you bastards!"

My men and I were pumped. I had hand-picked the soldiers by my side. Lots from the 31st, and others that had seen plenty of this stinking war's obscenities. Timing was going to be everything. If we didn't get this just right, our very own guns were going to kill us.

The guns went silent for a brief moment. This was it: the signal to advance. Our lines began to move forward. We had trained and practised for this like it was a well-rehearsed dance step. "Not too fast...don't get ahead of the barrage...easy now, wait for the Germans to pop up out of their rat holes. Locate the machine-gun nests, kill as many as possible—surprise is on our side—and then move on." The barrage advanced and started pounding more German real estate just ahead of us. Our boys behind were mopping up, diving into the vermin tunnels with pistols, bayonets, knives, or even shovels; whatever it took to get the job done.

To say the Huns were surprised was an understatement. Shock and fear were in their eyes as they succumbed to our onslaught. No one was supposed to be waiting outside their gunners' nests! This was a tactic they were just not ready for.

My gun was hot, the steam rising from it as we pushed forward. My men were still with me, most of them anyhow... These were Canada's best. Every one of them putting it all on the line. It literally came down to "DO or DIE!" The sound of war was all around us: the big guns screaming overhead, guns of every calibre incessantly firing, bullets constantly whizzing through the air. Shouting. Cursing. Crying and dying...

The acrid gun smoke entered my lungs like fiery coals; it felt like they were going to burst. Suddenly, my leg went numb. *Feels like I pulled a muscle,* I thought. *Got to keep going, can't let my men down. What's wrong with this damn leg?* Dropping to the ground, I managed to roll onto my good side. Sure enough, a red stain was forming on my trousers. *Shit! It looks like I took one just below my thigh!*

As I rolled to reach my belt to use as a tourniquet, I spotted sudden movement to my right. Three German rats crawled out of the ground, racing to reach their fixed machine gun, shouting and firing rifles and handguns in my direction. Luckily, in the confusion, their shots went wild. I knew that if just one of them made it to that weapon, I was a dead man!

"Oh no you don't, you assholes! Paul Bonenfant will not die today!"

Grabbing my gun, I rolled again, the pain now pouring into my body, and at the same time adrenalin pumping wildly! A short burst from my gun brought the first one down, his arms flapping like a goose's wings as he tumbled. The second dived for cover, but I thought I tagged him. He cursed and called me some kind of "pig dog" in German. The last one had dived into the nest and was bringing the gun to bear right at me.

I pulled the trigger of my own gun. Nothing. The damn thing had jammed! No time to pull out my sidearm. I rolled as fast and hard as I could. My wounded leg felt like a branding iron was burning on my skin. The ground I had just rolled from was chewed up in a spray of rock and dirt. My sidearm was now in my hand. As I pulled the trigger, my father's voice rang in my ears. "If you're not going to hit what you're aiming at, don't shoot! You dumb buggers!"

My bullet hit that fellow right in the middle of his forehead. Exploding brains and gore flew out the back of his skull. Gasping for breath now, I saw another soldier leap from his cover and start running at me with a rifle and fixed bayonet. He screamed and cursed as I put a bullet into his chest.

Strangely, the war sounds were fading now; all I could hear was my breathing and the pounding of my heart. Tired now...so very...very tired...then...BLACKNESS.

How much time had passed was anyone's guess. Could have been months or years for all I knew. The void I had been in was neither warm nor cold. How do you describe nothingness? What is time, anyhow? At first, I began to hear buzzing, sort of like a beehive up close, very low, then slowly getting louder.

Now I could hear voices, muffled and incoherent. Louder now...and then it hit me.

PAIN! Hot searing PAIN! I let out what I thought was a blood-curdling scream! "What the hell?!" Did those crazy quack doctors cut off my legs? If that were the case, then whoever was responsible would feel the sting of my blade! Why can't I open my eyes?

Out of the grey mist, I heard a voice. "Yeah, I am right! I knew it! That tough old Frenchman just moaned!" said the voice.

"Impossible!" said a different voice. "I'll be damned; some guys just won't quit! Quick! Get me some of that morphine! This soldier has a chance! The pain must be excruciating!"

"Silly bugger! I wasn't going to waste good morphine on a dead man! Had to cut a lot of flesh to dig that bullet out and the loss of blood was copious!"

"Wheel him into the other room! He just might make it!"

"So...what took you so long?" I managed to croak.

Joey just looked at me and grinned. "My big brother once again had to show everyone it's not that easy to kill a Bonenfant, eh? You scared the shit out of me! With all the casualties and confusion, it took me days to find you. I honestly thought I would be looking for a corpse. From the sounds of things, the medics thought you were just another dead soldier taking up valuable space in their field hospital too! I'm really glad you're a tough old bastard, Paul. I really am." His eyes misted up. "Yes, you're going home, back to England and Bea, just as soon as I can make it happen."

"Careful who you're calling an old bastard! Uncle Joey... that's the best news you could have brought me. I can't wait," I said with a weak smile.

"What...? What did you call me? Paul, you old dog! Is it true? Bea's having a baby?" Joey asked.

"She was. At least, just before we decided to reclaim Vimy she was." My voice was a bit louder than a whisper.

Now we were both grinning. "What a day this has turned out to be... My dead brother is alive, and I'm almost an uncle! Damn! Life is finally starting to look better and better! By the way, Paul, there are going to be some medals coming your way. I have also been told that if I found you alive, your rank would change too. You and your men were incredible! History will show that this was one of Canada's greatest military victories! We stood shoulder to shoulder and did what no one else could do. The war is a far cry from being over, but we got a lot accomplished. Heinie is watching his ass now!"

"Joey, I don't care about the medals. Just get me home to my family. By now Bea must have heard about Vimy Ridge; she needs to know that I'm alive, I'm coming home, and I love her! I need to get to my precious, darling wife!"

"I've got it handled, Paul. Just concentrate on healing." Joey waited as I fell asleep, still grinning.

Chapter Nine

IT SEEMED LIKE it was taking forever. Getting stabilized enough to move from the field hospital, being transported from the front, and then finally by ship back to England. All the while counting the moments until I could gaze upon that beautiful girl from Lancashire. I wanted nothing more to do with war or killing or politics anymore. Home was where I was going. Beatrice Bonenfant was my home!

I woke from a drug-induced sleep in the hospital and was certain that I was still dreaming. This angel stood over me, held my face with both her hands, and as the tears rolled down her cheeks, gently spoke to me. "Wake up, you big ox...we still have a lot of living to catch up on."

I will never forget that moment. Life was good again.

The days of recovery were interesting, to say the least. My physical wounds healed quickly, probably due to the fact that I had everything to look forward to. I was alive, I had a beautiful wife, and we had a baby on the way.

The mental scars, however, were another thing; they were still open and raw.

Nightmares, severe sweats, and those terrible war memories kept me awake most nights. I felt like I was losing my mind. The doctors said it was "shell shock" or "battle fatigue" and that it would eventually subside. They said the best cure was to get back into it as soon as possible; "Just like falling off a horse," they said.

I told them they were full of shit! With Joey pulling some strings, I was allowed to recuperate at home. The things I wanted most were rest, quiet, and relaxation, at least for a while. I knew that as soon as I was able, they would send me back into that hell. My amazing wife sensed all this and turned our home into a sanctuary of sorts. We avoided conversations about the war, instead focusing on our impending arrival. I started really getting my strength back. Long walks and fresh air were the new orders.

Somehow Joey managed to escape the war from time to time and stayed with us in our flat whenever possible. He became a help for both of us. Bea found him to be a real friend; she remarked, "Joey is the brother with all the empathy and compassion; he's very easy to talk to." She also told me I could take a few lessons from my charming brother. I was just happy everyone was getting along so well.

I was still amazed that my brother was in such demand with the military hierarchy. His close associates were some of the most powerful men of our time.

Extremely secretive, all he would say was, "I will tell you everything when this craziness is over; for now, you will just have to trust me." And I did.

I had been told by my war buddies that pregnant women were somehow much more interested in sex than usual. The consensus was that as they were already knocked up, there was no longer any concern about anything, and they could really enjoy themselves. Of course, when men talk of such things, it's usually a lot of swagger and embellishment, so I never really thought much about it, chalking it up as a lot of crap.

In our case, my dear wife always seemed ready to enjoy a roll in the hay and never did hold back. This, though, was different. She was insatiable. Now she had become the instigator and needed very little coaxing. Her adventurous spirit took over, and I really never knew what to expect.

Our daily ritual was a casual walk to a nice little neighbourhood park about a mile from our home. We would rest on one of the many sitting benches and just enjoy the flowers, birds, and each other's company.

On this particular glorious day, we strolled along hand in hand, nodding to passersby and making small talk. As there was a chill in the air, she had worn her heavier coat, one that buttoned right up and came down to her calves. She had let this one out, for obvious reasons.

Arriving at our favourite bench, we sat as always, my right arm around her shoulders to keep her close, holding her hand with the other.

"Paul," she said with a smile, "could you reach into my pocket and get my gloves? My hands are cold."

"Funny, they don't feel cold," I replied. So I reached into her pocket—no gloves. "Bea, there's a hole in your pocket; you probably lost them."

"Reach deeper," she said with a giggle. To my absolute surprise and delight, she was completely naked beneath that big coat.

"You are incorrigible, Bea," I whispered in her ear.

"What...you don't like what you're touching?" she said.

"Of course I do," I replied as I gently caressed her protruding tummy.

Bea changed her position slightly and leaned her head back as I softly began stroking her nether region, my hand still in her pocket. "That's it, Paul...slow and steady...we're not in any rush, are we?"

"Nope," I replied, "just don't ask me to stand up."

She laughed. The rosy hue of her cheeks wasn't from the cool air.

"Uh-oh, Bea, here come those two spinster sisters from down the block. Now what?" I whispered, my hand still in her pocket.

"Relax, Paul. Here's your chance to demonstrate to me how cool you can be in battle," she giggled.

"Well hello, you two love birds," the one named Martha said as she approached. "I see you are enjoying the glorious day, just as we are... Beautiful little spot, isn't it?"

"It certainly is, Martha, I have to agree, delightfully so," I replied with a grin.

"Paul, you seem to be recovering admirably, and Bea, you are positively glowing, dear! Motherhood seems to agree with you."

"Why thank you, you are too kind!" Bea replied. "And all is well with you two?"

"Oh my, yes, my sister and I are on our way to the pub. Would you care to come join us?"

"Ah...no, not today, Martha, thank you anyhow. My husband is feeling quite stiff right now. You know, the war wounds and all...must be the slight chill in the air, right dear?"

Trying hard to stifle a laugh, I replied, "Yes, I'm feeling a bit down today, so we'll have to pass." I gave Bea an imperceptible love poke as she coughed to create a diversion.

"Well, it was so nice talking to you two. Please come over for tea soon, okay? Ta-ra for now," and then they were on their way.

We waited until they were out of earshot and then couldn't stop laughing. "'Quite stiff,' you say, Bea? I'm rock-hard now!"

"Yes, I noticed you didn't uncross your legs at all," she said.

"You are a rascal, Bea! Seems like there's a lot more moisture in your pocket!" I laughingly replied.

"You know, Paul, there's probably room for another finger down there in that pocket." Her voice took on that familiar, telltale husky sound.

"Okay, you vixen." I quickly looked up and down the path. "Then I suggest we need to get home and properly take care of things!"

"I'm yours to command, kind sir!" Giggling again, Bea asked if I wanted to carry the umbrella in front of me on the way back. What a great day this was!

A few days later, there was Joey, sitting on the front stoop with an envelope on his lap as we came back from one of our regular walks. "Oh look, Paul; there's Joey," Bea said as we approached the house. "What a nice surprise!"

Not saying anything, I looked straight ahead at my brother as we got close. I knew by the look on Joey's face that this wasn't a social call.

"How's my big brother and his beautiful wife?" Joey quipped, his smile suddenly turning sombre.

"What's in the envelope, Joe?" I asked.

"Let's go inside; we need to talk," Joey replied.

"Oh no! I knew this day was coming," said Bea, her voice quivering. "I'd better put on some tea."

When we were alone in the sitting room, Joey began to speak in a low voice. "I pulled every string I could, Paul, called in favours like you wouldn't believe. This war is dragging on incessantly; my superiors want to see this damn thing over with. There's another big push, and they need your special talents to organize the 'ghost squads' again. You are to report for duty in two days at the old barrack site."

"Joe, I can't! Not now; you know how close Bea is!"

"Paul, this is not a request. This is orders from the top brass. Paul, I'm sorry!" The conflict was evident in his voice and features. "Many of your old squads are either dead or disabled. The ones left are relying on you to take charge and get the replacements trained and ready to roll out again in a couple of months. You will be operating incognito again, and your rank will be captain with the full backing of the CEF. Whatever you need is there at your disposal.

My superiors know you get results, and that's what they want. Your country needs you again, Paul!"

My eyes flashed, my temples pulsed, and my fists clenched. Stepping back, Joey looked like he didn't know what to expect.

"Okay, you two, how bad is it?" Bea asked with concern in her voice as she entered the room with the tray of tea.

"Everything is fine, Bea," I lied. "It's just a training school, but I am going to be gone for a while again." I saw the sadness and fear in her eyes. "I don't have any choice, darling. Like I have said many times before, the Army owns me until this shitty war is done." I glared at Joey.

Chapter Ten

SOME OF THE highest-ranking military and political men of the day were assembled. With the call to attention, the large room became quiet. Joey spoke first, explaining the importance of this top-secret training location and the group's ultimate mission. Then he introduced the different specialists, who would be giving hands-on training in various combat fields to each soldier.

I stood grim-faced and stoic as Joey presented me to the assembly. All was quiet as they waited for my words. I slowly walked along the front and looked each man in the face as they still stood to attention. I wasn't sure what I was going to say, but I felt the anger and intensity building.

"Many of you men have fought alongside me before. I am indeed proud to again be in your company. You others are hand-picked replacements for those who came first and are now dead. Most of us will not live to see this war end. All of us will be put in harm's way. I promise you all, here and now, I will do my best to keep you alive as long as possible. The training that you are about to receive will be your salvation. Every technique and skill you learn is of the utmost importance. Strive for perfection! Our only hope is to do our jobs well and help end this damn war quickly!

"We're headed once again into hell itself. Do not underestimate the enemy. They are trying just as hard as us to survive and live another day. Their lives are as important to them as ours are to us. I want you to feel ANGER! I want you to feel PAIN! We are all so tired of this 'War to end all Wars!' It's all a load of CRAP!

"The politicians, the aristocrats, the clergy, and the businessmen profiting on both sides have to be stopped. Unfortunately, they won't be on the front lines. Their soldiers will be, and we have to kill them to end this carnage. You will be the most efficient killers of our time, and for that, I am truly sorry."

As I turned to leave, it was deathly silent. Then thundering applause began. I found my seat beside Joey and felt my fists clench once again. Joey and the brass were stunned, looking back and forth at each other and then at me. Obviously, they didn't like the straightforward talk and candour.

Joey got up, said something, and introduced another man. Sitting down, he leaned over and whispered to me, "Where did you learn to talk like that, big brother?"

"I told the truth, and these men know it," I replied.

"Paul, your words are going to ruffle a lot of feathers. I don't know if those were the smartest things to say."

As I leaned into Joey, I replied, "FUCK THEM, Joe! What are they going to do, send me to the front? Let's get busy, these soldiers have got a lot to learn!"

The days and weeks flew by as the intense training took place. Specialized scenarios for night and day were created. The men were taught to think and react quickly. Their hand-to-hand combat skills grew; everything from guns and knives to shovels were lethal weapons in their grasp.

Lessons in the art of camouflage were also incredible. We had enlisted some Apache Indians from the desert to teach the men how to become almost invisible in daylight as well as night. Amazing transformations took place. Our soldiers became cunning, stealthy predators.

We were confined to these remote well-hidden barracks. Only the top brass were allowed in and out. Joey, though, basically came and went as he pleased. I still for the life of me could not understand his close connection with these powerful men. I knew it wasn't only through the military; his influence was everywhere. It was as if he belonged to some secret society that transcended regular boundaries.

Oh well, my task was to get these soldiers ready for war, not speculate on fanciful ideas. I was grateful for the interchange of letters between Bea and myself (courtesy of my little brother). She was my lifeline to sanity. She told me she was doing her best. The birth of our first child, a healthy baby girl she had named Samantha, had apparently been a bit late. Nothing to worry about but she described these days as "difficult."

I pleaded with Joe to give me even a couple of days with her. He explained that it was not possible. She had the best doctor available and was doing just fine. Too much was at stake and that no one must discover this top-secret location and mission.

Finally, we were done. The training was over, for the time being. Our men were ready; the students had become masters. The program was being closely watched; if it proved successful, it would continue and be expanded.

Joe was now appointed Commander-in-Chief, with responsibility for intelligence-gathering along the entire Western Front. No official rank or recognition was given, as we didn't actually exist. My job was as one of the liaison captains. Once orders were issued, I oversaw operations and missions in my area. It was a stressful and tense position. I hated the constant life-and-death decisions.

Eventually, I was allowed some time off. I headed home to two beautiful females, my darling wife and our precious newborn daughter. It had been a while since I stepped over the threshold of our little flat. And believe it or not, I found myself a bit nervous.

What kind of welcome could this absentee husband and father expect? I knocked on the door and turned the handle.

There they were, my beautiful girls, Beatrice and baby Samantha. Tears rolled down Bea's cheeks as she smiled and stood up to kiss me.

"It's about time, Paul; we've been waiting. Joey told us you were coming home today. Meet your daughter, Samantha."

My eyes began misting, and words finally made it out of my mouth. "God, Bea...she's as pretty as a spring day! You did a great job, sweetheart. I'm so sorry I wasn't here for you!"

"Here, hold her in your arms," my wife said.

"I don't know, Bea...what if I drop her, or don't do something right?"

"Just support her head, like this; you'll be fine. It's time for the two of you to get to know each other. I need to sit down; come over by the couch…"

I realized Bea had become quite pale, and weak-looking. Her sister, Liz, had been standing off to the side. She finally spoke. "Paul, she had a rough time…lost a lot of blood and only just managed in the last few days to get out of the hospital bed and come home. We were all so worried." I saw the concern on her face.

"Oh, don't be carrying on, Liz; the doctor says everything will be fine. I just have to be careful for a while. Really, you two. Now that Daddy's home, everything is going to be better," she said.

I was so overjoyed, holding that little darling, and at the same time worried about Bea. "I didn't know, Bea…I honestly didn't know. This damn war—when is it ever going to end!" I exclaimed.

"Paul, watch your language. We have a baby in the room!" she said with a grin.

Our lives are going to be changing now, I thought.

Liz pulled a chair up and poured some tea for everyone. Samantha made some cooing noises, and we all laughed. Amidst the horror of what was happening, this new life brought hope to all of us.

After about a week had gone by, I awoke with a start. A faint rustling noise was coming from the kitchen. It wasn't Bea, as she was blissfully sound asleep beside me. Samantha was safe in her bassinet, her eyes open, making those sweet little cooing sounds and kicking her feet.

My senses were on full alert as I crept down the hall, the "toothpick" deftly ready in my left hand. The right hand must always be free. I made no sound whatsoever.

There he was, as brazen as could be, reaching into the upper cupboard. "You know, Joey, you could easily get yourself killed coming in here like that," I said quietly.

Seemingly not startled, Joey turned around and asked where Bea kept that big fry pan. "I managed to acquire coffee, a dozen eggs, and some ham." He grinned. "It's just about sunup, and I didn't want to wake you two, so I used my key and let myself in. Sorry if I startled you, big brother! This morning we feast!" He laughed.

"You crazy loon!" I laughed back. With wartime rationing going on, this was a special treat!

The breakfast turned out great. Liz showed up out of the blue, bringing over some fresh scones. Bea added her flapjack recipe to the mix and Joey was right, it really was a feast! Our family was definitely coming together.

Chapter Eleven

THE NEXT DAY Joey and I left. He had a car and driver pick us up. Inside the car, he began to reveal what the next mission entailed. Intelligence had found out that the Germans had developed a modern gas mask, far superior to ours, and we were desperate to get our hands on it. Just because they were our enemy didn't mean we didn't admire their intellect and manufacturing skills.

All attempts to acquire one had so far failed. We needed to snag one, now.

Thousands of Allied lives depended on it.

"So, Paul, how do you want to handle this? It's your call," he said.

After getting all the details, I told him, "Joe, my chances are best if I go in by myself; a group of four or five men will be noticed. I know I can blend in easily. I will need some time to tune up my German skills. Give me a few days to lay it all out for you. Okay?"

"Whatever you want, you got it, big brother. I can make it happen!" he replied.

"You amaze me, Joe! I know, I know...I am not going to ask any more questions. Just promise me you'll look after Bea and Samantha if anything goes wrong," I said.

"That goes without saying, Paul," Joey replied.

The actual entry point was miles up the front. This was the best spot, as there was still lots of cover. The war hadn't decimated the land here yet. I would do what I had to do: formulate a plan once on the other side, retrieve the package, and get back. There was no tight completion date; a password known only to three of my best men on our side of the line would be my ticket back. The added risk with this plan was the possibility of getting shot by one of our own soldiers.

Things were going rather well. After a few days, I had managed to get into the little town that held the German military storage facility. I determined that the building was well-guarded. A frontal attempt was out of the question. They had roving soldiers at each set of doors.

This is going to be a bigger problem than anticipated, I thought to myself. The weak spot was the roof; incredibly, no one was up there. So, how to get up there? In the back, believe it or not, was a metal ladder attached to the wall about ten feet from the ground. Now I knew this was going to be possible! My camouflage and stealth training was really going to be tested.

I set about collecting local foliage and vegetation from the surrounding area, all done well away from view and mostly under cover of darkness. I was creating my own bush suit. The Apache Indians were the best in the world at this, and we had conscripted two of them into our training program back in England to teach us this technique. As long as a man was patient and crept along extremely slowly, moving only when no one was directly looking at him, he could come within a few feet of a destination without arousing suspicion.

I actually looked like a bush when the suit was completed. Now, to wait until darkness...

Upon reaching the back side of the building, I calmly waited until the guard was sleepily wandering in the opposite direction. In the darkness, the bush silently scrambled up to the roof. A couple of skylights were up there, alright, and it looked like they had been propped open to allow for some ventilation.

This is too easy, I thought. I let myself down via a rope I had acquired in town and saw hundreds of stacked wooden crates. Now to quietly pry one open with my "toothpick" and see what was in there.

The light from the open skylights was enough to show me I had hit the mother lode. Each crate contained about ten masks. I only needed one! I placed the gas mask in the empty sack I had brought along for that very purpose, putting the lid back in place afterward. Smiling to myself, I turned to grab onto the rope.

And there he was, a low throaty growl emanating from his mouth. *Shit,* I thought, *I knew this was too easy!* The old dog just stood there, looking at this slow-moving bush and growling. Who knows what was going through his head.

Inspiration struck; I slowly reached into my pocket and pulled out some leftover schnitzel. Unwrapping it from the wax paper, I held it out for the mutt. He looked at it and then quickly took the meat and slunk off to a corner to eat.

Time to move! The bush shinnied up the rope. Waiting for the right moment, I climbed down on the dark side and very slowly moved to cover. Every instinct tells you to run! But you don't dare. "Just as slow as coming in, you go out!" My Apache mentor had trained me well.

Everything had gone great! And I didn't have to kill anyone. The thought even crossed my mind to take a room in town. *No, Paul! Don't push your luck!* I found a spot in the brush and caught some shut-eye.

My re-entry point on the line was just ahead. So far I was in the clear; some quick manoeuvers of my wire-cutters and I was through. It was pitch black, and there was no moon—a perfect night for travelling. I knew I was now in Allied territory.

Just up ahead something moved, and I could see the small orange glow of someone's cigarette. "Stupid bastard!" I thought. "That's a perfect sniper target!" As I got closer, this dumbass sentry coughed. Well, maybe I could teach this peckerhead a valuable lesson, and he just might live another day. *Wonder where my men are waiting; they can't be too far away*, I thought.

Creeping up behind the young soldier, I easily disarmed him and had him on the ground, my knee into his back.

A hand cupped around his mouth, I gruffly whispered in his ear, "Stay down and listen carefully! I'm one of you. I need you to slowly stand and take me to your commanding officer. Make no mistakes now, or yes, I will kill you! Do you understand?" I asked menacingly.

Barely able to speak, he nodded and said a quiet, "Yes, sir!"

"Good, now get up and let's start walking," I said as I took the bullets out of his rifle. "Sorry, son, I can't take a chance on you accidently shooting me in the back," I explained.

About fifty yards ahead, another voice called out, "Halt, who goes there?"

"It's me, Mac. Everything's okay; I'm bringing in a prisoner."

"No shit!" was the reply. "I mean, what's the password?"

"Dumbass" correctly replied, and all of a sudden there were soldiers all around. My hands in the air, I explained that I needed to see whoever was in command.

The young pup named Mac decided to show off for his buddies and gave me a rifle butt to the stomach. "That's what German prisoners get from us, Heinie! You don't get to talk unless we let you!"

The other soldier finally stepped in and told him to back off and get word to the CO that they were bringing in a prisoner. I made a vow to myself that this Mac guy was going to eventually be taught a lesson.

The gunny sack with my stolen German gas mask was roughly taken and would be handed over to their Commanding Officer.

As I sat on a stump with my hands tied behind my back, the CO of this kindergarten class came over and explained that he had sent word of my capture down the line and that there should be a reply in a day or so. I had told him that my mission was top-secret and that he needed to alert a certain general as soon as possible.

"Best we can do, mister. Just be glad my men didn't shoot you! Why don't you just tell me what you need to speak to the general about? Maybe then I can untie you, and you'll feel a lot more comfortable?" he pressed.

I thought to myself, *That will never happen, you idiot!* As I sat there trying to remain calm, I wondered where the hell my men were. Something really strange was going on here.

The nincompoop CO eventually determined I wasn't a spy or a threat to his men and untied me. He said I would be watched closely, though. My guns would be returned when the right authorities arrived.

Two days went by. Finally, my men showed up with the necessary paperwork to get me released into their custody. When we were out of earshot, I angrily asked, "Where the hell were you guys?!"

Cody, the team leader and one of the best soldiers I had ever served with, explained that when no contact had been made after a few days, orders had come down that the mission was to be aborted. They were told to head down the line about twenty miles and wait for further instructions. He said, "Paul, we thought you were dead. Not one of us wanted to leave until we were sure, but the orders were clear: 'Abort mission now!'"

The explanation was logical, but somehow my gut wasn't satisfied. Well, the mission was a success regardless of the screw-up. Our boys would have a better chance of surviving a gas attack once we replicated the German technology. I felt good about the result.

Cody said my brother would be here in a couple of weeks and had said that he was glad I was still alive and that London had him tied up for a while. For now, my men and I were ordered back from the front and told to await further instructions.

I wanted desperately to get back to my family. It had been months now since I had seen Bea. Her letters had been sparse lately, but I had attributed that to the logistics of war. Finally, a mail pouch found its way to us. I grabbed the lone letter and sought out a quiet spot to read every word. She talked about the mundane goings-on in our neighbour-hood, her sisters' lives, and the weather.

Then she dropped the bombshell that we were about to be blessed with another child. She was now three months gone and could feel confident that things were progressing well. I exhaled as the written words turned into various thoughts in my mind. Feelings of unease started to churn in my gut. My wife pregnant again. *"Three months gone"; how can this be possible?* I thought. It had been at least that long since I was home, and we had abstained from anything too physical then because of her condition.

Surely one of us was mistaken...

I needed to get home! *Maybe Joe can pull some strings,* I thought. I sent an official dispatch to his liaison people.

Three days went by, and finally his reply showed up: "Will be there by week's end. Bringing some high-ranking friends. Field ceremony to award medals to my big brother. See you then. –Joe."

That's not what I wanted. They can shove their damn medals! I need to get home! I thought.

Chapter Twelve

T HE ENTOURAGE OF military vehicles came to a stop in front of the simple tent shack that served as our headquarters. Our CO stepped out to greet the parade of officials. Standing behind the tent wall, I saw my brother and some general get out of the last car. They had obviously been enjoying some alcoholic beverages; both had quite a glow.

"You're absolutely right, Joe! This war is all about protecting our way of life and our families! You got any children, Joe?" the affable general asked.

Joey, not thinking anyone else was within earshot, replied, "Well, sir, as a matter of fact, my sweet woman has just informed me she is in the family way, and I am just ecstatic!"

"Congratulations, Joe! You do sound pleased! The grand event is soon, I take it?" he asked.

"No, sir, probably another five or six months to go yet. Everything is going well, though. As soon as this medal presentation is done, I'm headed home."

Home...? Home...?! My heart was pounding so fast I thought it would blow up. It was difficult to breathe. My fists were clenched so tightly they were white. I could not believe what I had just heard come out of my brother's mouth!

The realization screamed into my mind that I was not supposed to survive this last mission. It had been a neat and tidy way to get me out of the way. Everything fit! Betrayal and deceit by the two people I loved most in this world. Nothing could have prepared me for this! My rage was out of control. As I bounded around the side of that tent shack, I saw fear on Joey's face. He knew I had heard it all.

"General, here's the hero we came to see: my brother Paul!" he was able to quip just as he managed to step back a bit.

The inhuman snarl that emitted from my flying form was cause for the general to shout out, "Look out, Joe!" Too late—my right-handed blow hit Joey's jaw like a sledgehammer. The crunch of bones snapping was probably the last thing Joe heard as he crumpled to the ground.

I felt arms grab me and then took a rifle butt to the head. There it was again, that empty but all-too-familiar black void. I have no idea how long I was out.

The first thing I felt was an intense, throbbing pain. My head had been loosely wrapped with some kind of bandage. My arms and legs were shackled. I lay on an army-issue cot. One ear was totally deaf, and I couldn't get my eyes to focus. The hum of voices suddenly got louder, and I tried to remember what had happened.

Then the horrible memory came flooding back. I desperately wanted to return to the black void, where nothing could touch me. My body hurt like hell, but my heart was totally broken. How could they have done this to me? I lay there not moving, hoping I would die.

Eventually, an army doctor came to see if I was still alive. Once he knew I was conscious, he told me I was one lucky bastard; everyone had wanted to shoot me immediately. He went on to say that the CO had told everyone I would be dealt with quickly. Striking a superior officer was an automatic death sentence in a time of war. The doc then went on to say that, curiously, I had been ordered to be returned under heavy guard to London for a court marshal.

"Who the hell are you, soldier?" he asked.

I dully looked back at him and said nothing. My life was over.

The doc was right. I was handcuffed and put in leg-irons. Three burly no-nonsense guards were to escort me to some military prison in England. I didn't really care anymore.

The accommodations were cold and damp. Concrete walls, steel bars, a cot, toilet, and basin made up the decor. No other prisoners were in the building I was in. Just me. It was a couple of weeks before my case was to be heard. The tribunal was being presided over by a small group of high-ranking officers. I recognized one of them as having been present at some of the top-secret mission locations. He was actually not a bad fellow, I had thought.

I was brought in and told to remain standing as the trumped-up charges were read: "insubordination," "absent without leave," etc., etc., and finally "attempted murder."

All a total sham, with no resemblance to a fair trial. There was no discussion of legal representation. They skipped directly through to the pronouncement of the sentence. Since this was the army, they could do whatever they wanted.

They began by telling me that as a decorated hero and because of my exemplary service to my country, the mandatory death sentence had been waived. However, because of the secrecy of our clandestine "ghost squads," a problem existed. In order to maintain that secrecy and not jeopardize the war effort, I was to be incarcerated until the war's end.

My service records would all be rewritten. My rank would be stripped and shown as an enlisted private. My name would be formally changed to "Alex Bonenfant" on all documentation. Paul Bonenfant would never have served in the Canadian military. I would not be allowed to return to Canada until all CEF members had returned home.

After the lengthy sentencing tirade had ended, I was asked if I wished to speak.

Looking slowly at each officer in that group, I replied in an even voice, "No, sir."

That was it. I was led back to my cell.

The accompanying guard quietly said to me, "You played it well, sir; they were baiting you, and it would not have worked out in your favour."

I knew it was going to be difficult to maintain my sanity. I knew I had done everything that the Army had asked of me and more. A vendetta was obviously in place here, and I had a good idea of who was behind it all...

Chapter Thirteen

TWO YEARS LATER I was on a ship bound for Canada. The hostilities had ceased on November 11, 1918. It was now September of 1920.

As there was no further correspondence from Bea, I presumed she had been told I was dead. The anger I harboured for them both, and the military, was probably what had kept me alive all the time I was in prison. It felt good to be finally rid of England. I would never return to Europe again.

As the ship docked in Montreal, a new wave of despair took over. I realized I had wasted over seven years of my life. I had taken many lives in the name of king and country, and now here I was, an angry, burnt-out soldier with no past or even my real name anymore.

"Where do I go from here?" I thought. I decided I would eventually head back to where the adventure had all began...Calgary. The more distance from that dark hell I could put behind me, the better. Before that, though, I needed to visit the old farm in New Brunswick. I don't know why; it was just something I needed to do. I had been thinking about my parents lately, and it seemed like the right place to be for a while.

There was really nothing left there anymore, just some burnt-out buildings and neglected corrals. Overgrown fields and the forest reclaiming the land again. A lonesome wind was blowing, and a definite chill was in the air.

God, I wished I could talk to my old man again, feel the embrace of my mother, hear the chatter of my siblings at play. What had happened to my life? I needed to try to get my head straight again. The night sweats, horrible dreams, and voices...sometimes I felt it was too much to bear.

"So, are you a ghost come back to haunt my sister and me?" a voice from the bush hollered out. Startled, I jumped back and reached for the sidearm in my jacket that they had let me keep. "Easy, Paleface! If I wanted to hurt you, the ground would now be in your face. Or should I call you 'Night Puma'?"

As the figure emerged from the bushes, he let out a hearty laugh. "You know, that really was a dumb name my father gave you. I always thought you made as much noise as a moose at night. Thought you might be dead by now. Been a long time. My sister cries herself to sleep every night, you know."

"You are so full of shit, Jackson!" I said. "You still like to chatter on like an old woman!" We were both grinning from ear to ear now.

"It's good to see you, brother!" Jackson went on.

"Yeah, it has been a long time; got caught up in the damn war, you know," I explained.

"What you doing here? Going to start farming again?" Jackson asked.

"No, that's not going to happen, just visiting some old spirits. Thought maybe I could heal my brain a little bit..."

Jackson's eyes went wide. "Really, you talking to someone I know?"

"Could be..."

"This is a lonely place, Paul. How about you come back with me, spend some time, catch up, you know? My cabin is a few miles up the hill. We'll skin these rabbits I caught, eat, drink some whisky, and tell lies tonight."

"Why not!" I thought. "That sounds great. Lead the way, Jackson—that is, if you're not going to get us lost," I kidded him.

"White man thinks he's funny, eh?"

The cabin was small, but very cozy and warm. The main window overlooked a wooded ravine; a stream ran close by. Soon we had a stew pot cooking over the fire. Jackson brought out a jug, pulled the cork out, and passed it to me.

"Company first!" he cackled.

"You always had impeccable manners," I told him.

"What's 'impeccable' mean?" he asked.

"Means you are a good friend."

A big smile was on his face now. "My sister is married, has three kids, one more on the way, and drives her husband crazy. You dodged a bullet there!" We both laughed.

"Say hello for me, will you?" I asked.

"Sure thing," he replied. "Pass that jug, Paleface!"

As things turned out, this was just what the doctor ordered. Jackson insisted I stay the winter and help him work his trap-line. I told him I would, but come spring I thought I would head out west again. "It's a free country, friend—unless you're an Indian," he chuckled.

It seemed like old times. My nightmares calmed down some. Jackson prepared some herbs and crafted a magic talisman for me. He said that as long as I wore this talisman and took the herbs, it would help to stop the bad dreams and scare away the evil spirits. Couldn't hurt, so I did as he said.

Chapter Fourteen

CALGARY HADN'T CHANGED much since I had last seen it. Still had that bustling frontier flair going on. The thing that really felt best was the wide-open spaces and wonderfully clean air. Maybe if I breathed deep enough, I could finally expel the stink of that damn war from my lungs.

With very limited dollars in my pocket, I decided to treat myself to a couple of beers. I realized my next task was to find a job, and the best place to get information about that was the local watering hole.

The Palliser was one of the first hotels in Alberta to get a liquor licence now that Prohibition had been repealed. People were easy-going, open, and friendly. The consensus, though, was that work was scarce here. Too many men coming back from the war and very little going on. Most said I would have better luck up in the central part of the province, or even as far north as Edmonton.

I thanked the group of ranchers I had been sitting with and decided to leave. As I walked through the bar and was about to grab the big wooden door, a drunken voice bellowed out, "Paul, Paul...we thought you were dead; it's great to see you again!" At that, the entire group of ex-soldiers from his table stood up and offered a salute. The loudest of the group decided to tell the entire bar that here was a real-life war hero! Big-mouth went on to say so many of the 31st battalion owed me their lives. Taken by surprise and honestly glad to see these old comrades of mine, I agreed to sit and let them buy me a beer or three. I made a point of letting them know I couldn't stay long, though. Knowing that this was going to be a long and noisy night, I just didn't feel up to it.

After a couple of hours, I stood and bid them all farewell. Before leaving, one of the men slid a large bottle of whiskey into my coat pocket and grabbed my hand. Looking hard into my eyes, he wished me good luck. "We all owe you, Paul; if ever you need..."

"Yeah, yeah," I replied. "See you in the next war."

Walking down the street, I thought to myself that I had never corrected anyone as to my name change, or mentioned how the army had treated me. No need to stir the pot.

Finally, arriving down at the train station, I plunked some money down on the counter and asked, "How far will this take me?"

After a while, the kindly old gent said he could give me a ticket to Stettler. "Then Stettler it is, friend!" I replied.

It was dusk as the train pulled into the dusty little whistle stop. The only people to disembark were myself and a grizzled old rancher badly in need of a bath. Grabbing my two army-issue duffle bags off the train, I stepped down to the loading dock. Out of the corner of my eye, I spotted that same old codger, now wearing his weathered cowboy hat and slicker. He was struggling to slide a steamer trunk off the train car onto a cart.

Putting my bags down, I walked the short distance over and said to him, "You look like you could use a hand, buddy. Let me grab an end, and we'll get it on that wheeler."

Slowly looking up, he answered, "Much obliged, mister, been travelling for weeks now and I'm just about done in. You from around here?" he asked after we got his trunk moved.

"Nope," I replied, "never set foot here before."

"Soldier?" he enquired, looking me and my duffle bags over.

"Ex," I replied, "Looking for work."

"Not much happening here. Maybe check in at the Royal Hotel just down the block. Anything going on here, Ed Hart at the bar might be able to point you in the right direction."

"Thanks for the tip!" I replied.

The old fellow stretched out his hand and said, "Name's Garth."

Shaking his gnarled thick hand, I told him, "They call me Alex. Maybe our paths will cross again. You never know, Garth."

With that, I picked up my bags and headed to the Royal Hotel. It had been a long time since I had experienced a decent night's sleep. When exhaustion finally overtook me,

I could manage maybe two or three hours at most before the nightmares began.

Sometimes a loud noise would wake me, and I would immediately reach for my gun or my knife, or both, usually in a sweat, with my heart pounding furiously.

Thankfully, the military had returned my "toothpick," and it was securely strapped to my leg again. The revolver was in my duffle bag. This was courtesy of one of the sympathetic guards who looked out for me in prison. He suspected it might be a good idea for me to be armed now that I was no longer in the army. "Lots of trouble out there," he had said as he shook my hand goodbye.

This was going to be my new beginning and a fresh start. I desperately wanted the last eight years to be gone from my consciousness. During the day it actually wasn't too bad. But my demons came out at night and I was in hell all over, again and again and again!

The room I had been given was at the back of the hotel on the third floor. Just a bed, desk, chair, nightstand, and a window looking out over the back alley, with a shared bathroom down the hall. Although there wasn't anyone else around. I had enough money to rent it for a week.

Two days and two sleepless nights later, the depression and despair had become the worst ever. Having had nothing to eat except some jerky from one of my duffle bags, I was in rough shape. I remembered the bottle of whisky in my coat pocket and thought that might help. So I started to try to drink my troubles away.

Nothing helped—only delusions and confusion to now add to my paranoia. I couldn't even manage to pass out, tossing and turning on that lumpy bed. Soon the demons were back...there were the contorted faces of men I had killed...bleeding soldiers...screams of agony from my men dying. Some begging for their mothers.

Bullets and bombs exploding everywhere.

And amongst it all, my ex-wife and brother loudly laughing in my face. I knew it wasn't real, but even so, the noise and shouting wouldn't stop.

I just wanted it to end! The revolver seemingly jumped into my hand, and I stared at it. *Yes*, I thought. *Maybe that's the answer. It will finally be over!* No one would miss me. I could drift back into that non-existence, the black void I had been in so many times before as I recovered from my wounds. I turned the gun over and over in my hands. Why should I care anymore?

Suddenly, I heard a female voice and incessant knocking on the door. "Housekeeping, mister. I have to change the bedding and towels," she said politely. "May I come in?"

Angry at the intrusion, I shouted, "Go away! Leave me alone! I don't want any damn towels!"

The voice was quiet. She didn't say a thing, but I knew she was standing outside the door. To my surprise, she had the nerve to slowly push it open. In my drunken haze, I had never locked it. Was she crazy? What kind of woman would do something so foolhardy and dangerous?

The door swung in with a creaking noise. I could see she was trembling. In her arms, she cradled the clean linens. She stared, kind of mesmerized, just taking in the whole scenario.

"What's the matter, girl? Are you stupid?" I gruffly said, with my bloodshot eyes.

Looking at the gun on the table and then at me, she quietly spoke. "Mister, if you are planning on doing yourself in, it's going to be me that will have to clean up the mess. I really don't think you are being fair. You should go somewhere else and take the coward's way out, if that's what you have to do."

I just sat there, dumbfounded more than anything. Neither one of us spoke for what seemed like forever. A silent, awkward moment frozen in time.

Then, slowly and calmer now, I said, "You're right, ma'am, but nothing in life is ever fair. I promise not to do myself in right now."

She backed out of the doorway still clutching those linens. I got up and swung the creaking door closed. Sitting back down on the lone chair, my hands began to shake, and tears welled up in my eyes. *What have I become?* I thought. *I'm NOT just another burnt-out soldier. I'm a man, a damn good man. I want to live! All through that stinking war, I fought every day just to survive, and I'm not giving up yet!*

With that, I grabbed the near-empty bottle and smashed it against the wall. Then I immediately thought, *I'm going to have to clean that up!*

The room was silent now; the only sound I heard was my steady breathing. Looking out the small hotel window,

I noticed the sun shining through the curtains, highlighting the tiny, floating dust particles. Reaching over, I pushed open the window and smelled the clean, fresh air.

An unfamiliar, peaceful feeling came over me. This was my new day. Yes, I was going to make it! I would take on those bastard demons one by one! I wasn't going to give up! I was going to survive!

Exhausted now, I fell down on that lumpy bed. For the first time in a long while, I slept soundly.

Chapter Fifteen

M Y EYES FINALLY opened to a beautiful morning. After a thorough wash, shave, and clean-up, I needed to find something to eat. The café attached to the hotel was just opening. The lady from the front desk greeted me with a friendly "Hello." She and her husband owned the hotel.

From the kitchen, a familiar voice hollered out, "Lydia, where did you put those napkin holders?" As she came into the café section, she saw me and immediately her face went red. Stammering a bit now, she managed to say, "Good morning, sir, it's good to see you up and about. Lydia, this is the gentleman I was telling you about."

Suddenly, Lydia's countenance changed, and she was quickly at the younger woman's side. She placed a protective arm around her shoulder. "Mister, you have a lot of explaining to do!" she said. "I should have you thrown out! My sister was scared out of her wits! Lena, go and fetch Art from the bar," she said.

"Please, ladies, I mean no harm," I explained. "Your sister here saw me at the lowest point in my life, and I apologize profusely! I owe you an impossible debt, and I thank you for probably saving my miserable hide. If I could turn back the clock, I would. My name is Alex…Alex Bonenfant, and I offer you my heartfelt gratitude!"

My outstretched hand was hesitatingly taken, and Lydia's sister replied, "My name is Lena."

"Hello, Lena," I said gently. "Would it be okay to buy you a coffee and hopefully start over? I need to explain some things, if you would let me."

"Well, I suppose I could take a bit of a break; there's no one really here yet," she replied.

Lydia's arm came down from around her sister's shoulder and a loud "Harrumph!" indicated her displeasure. "Lena, I am right over here at the counter, and if I holler, Art will be here in a moment!"

"It's okay, sis, I'll be fine," she replied in a steady voice. We sat at a nearby table.

"I'm glad to see you are a man of your word, Alex," she said.

Puzzled, I replied, "How so?"

"You promised me you wouldn't do yourself in…for the moment, anyhow." An easy-going smile was now on her face.

Chuckling, I replied, "I deserved that. I can also promise you that I will never again entertain the idea of doing something so stupid again. I was rude and obnoxious to you. I am very sorry. Please believe me when I tell you I am not a coward, Lena. I've faced many a difficult situation in the past and survived," I said.

Sitting straight across from me and staring into my eyes, she stated, "I believe you, Alex," still with a mischievous grin.

I felt a wide smile spread across my face. *She is so easy to talk to*, I thought to myself—and very easy on the eyes.

We made small talk for a while, and Lena asked if I was hungry. "I'm famished," was my reply. "The aromas coming from the kitchen are driving me crazy."

With that, she was up. "Bacon, sausage, eggs, pancakes?"

"Yes, yes, and yes!"

Lydia, still watching close by, bluntly asked me if I had enough money to pay for breakfast.

"Yes, ma'am, I do, but probably not much more than that. Being honest, I'm pretty well tapped out, and I need to find work."

Looking me up and down, she asked, "So what are you good at?"

"I was a farmer and a fair carpenter before the war. So I can build, repair, or fix just about anything. The past five years or so I was employed by the Canadian Expeditionary Forces. Not that knowing my way around weapons is really an asset," I replied.

"Hmm... When you finish your breakfast, come around to the bar next door, and I'll introduce you to my husband, Art. You never know."

"Thank you, ma'am, I really appreciate the chance to show your family I'm a decent guy!"

"Nothing's for sure, and don't call me 'ma'am' anymore; my name is Lydia."

Offering her my outstretched hand, I said "Thank you, Lydia."

It was your typical small-town saloon. The long, stand-up bar was nothing spectacular. Lots of cigarette burns in the well-worn, wooden top. Old, mismatched chairs and tables in need of repair completed the décor. A distinct odour of tobacco and beer permeated the place. Lydia and her husband were behind the counter, unpacking some boxes.

As I approached, Lydia acknowledged me and then spoke to her spouse, "Art, here's the gentleman I told you about. Well, I best be getting back to the café; Lena will be needing my help now. You two can talk in private."

I offered my hand in greeting.

Replying with a firm handshake, Art motioned me over to a table. "So, my wife says you're looking for work?" he said.

"Yes, sir, and I am willing to do anything to earn my keep. I am mighty handy at woodwork, I can do repairs, sweep floors, paint, whatever you need done," I replied.

"Heard you were a soldier. Learn any skills that might help me improve my hotel?"

"Well, not directly, sir, but I do know how to take orders."

Art laughed and said, "That's a good quality. My wife kind of rules the roost around here and does her best to keep things on track, if you know what I mean," he replied.

"Yes, sir, she seems most capable."

"She is, and I don't know what I would do without her. You a drinker?" he asked.

"No, not normally, but yesterday I'm afraid I made a fool of myself in front of your sister-in-law, Lena. I have begged her forgiveness. It will never happen again. I don't appreciate drunkenness, Art, and I respect the power of alcohol."

"Well," said Art, "I pay $1.50 a day plus room and board. Any tips you acquire are split fifty-fifty with the house. There's a shed out back with a cot in it. You can live there. It needs some attention, but it's okay. I'll get Lena to clean it up and make it livable. Wintertime, I'll let you stay in one of the rooms upstairs in the back. You interested? Yes or no?"

"Yes, sir! You got yourself an employee. When do I start?" I asked.

"See that apron over there, Alex? Grab it and that mop and bucket and get to work. This place smells like hell! By the way, don't call me 'sir'; name's Art. You work hard, I'll treat you well. Screw me around, and you're gone! Do we understand each other?"

"Yes, si...I mean, Art. You won't be sorry. Thanks for the chance!"

I saw a pretty little face smiling at me by the doorway behind Art. She gave me a half-wave and was gone. "I'll be damned," I thought, "Stettler is turning into a very interesting place."

By the end of the afternoon, the old wooden floors looked great. Some of the locals had started to wander in, got their beers, found familiar tables, and begun the difficult task of solving the world's problems.

It occurred to me that I hadn't thought about the war all day. The grumbling in my stomach, though, reminded me I hadn't eaten since morning. As if reading my mind, Art came over to where I was working. "Looking good, Alex. That floor never shone like that before!" he remarked.

"Go find Lena and she will show you where the help eat out back."

"Hello, soldier boy! So how's your first day of honest work going?" Lena asked.

Something about her easy-going way made me smile... that hadn't happened in a long time.

"Today was okay, but now it just got so much better!"

Giggling, she replied, "Why, Alex Bonenfant, are you flirting with me?"

"Lena, I wouldn't take that liberty until I got to know you better! I'm just looking forward to some of your delicious cooking." A big grin spread across my face.

Laughing, she replied, "Why, you rascal, you are a charmer! I think I like that! Is it okay if I join you? I haven't had my supper yet," she said.

"I couldn't ask for better company, Lena," I said. *Yes, Stettler is looking better and better!* I thought to myself.

After about an hour of great food and scintillating company, I reluctantly told Lena I had to get back to the bar, as Art had asked if I could help out with the evening crowd.

"See you again, soldier boy!" She smiled.

"I sure hope so!" I replied.

The bar shut down at 10:00 p.m. I paid close attention to what Art was teaching me. We seemed to hit it off; he commented that I was a good worker and asked me if I was planning on hanging around for a while. My reply was that

I had no intention of moving on, at least not in the near future. "Stettler could get very comfortable," I told him.

Chapter Sixteen

THE FIRST WEEK went by very quickly. I moved out of the room in the back of the hotel and into the shed by the back alley. With a happy enthusiasm, Lena had taken on the job of making that shed livable for the Royal Hotel's newest employee, even finding some curtains for the lone window. When it was done, it was like a little playhouse.

She made a point of not being alone in there with me, though. Her older sister watched us like a hawk and certainly didn't want people talking. We still had our meals together in the hotel, and a genuine friendship had begun.

As time went on, I learned that her family had immigrated to Canada about fifteen years ago from a country called Bessarabia. It was close to the Black Sea, and the life they had left there was far better than theirs here in this harsh new land. The "Mix" family of five girls and three boys had not been prepared for Canada and nearly perished during their first winter.

The best part of each day was when I could spend time with Lena. She was always happy and seemed to look for the best in people. Me, on the other hand...well, I had been through hell in the war. The worst war in the planet's history! It would take me a lifetime to be positive about humanity again.

The nightmares still happened, although not as often or as graphic. I definitely was healing. Every spare moment I had, I devoted to keeping busy. I made it my goal to repair and rebuild every chair and table in that old bar.

Art couldn't have been happier. He remarked that the place was beginning to look prosperous. "We may have to begin charging more for beer; we are getting busier!" (Of course, that didn't happen.) Art promoted me to "assistant bar manager," with a small raise in pay, and began teaching me the ropes.

I had made it a point not to drink alcohol anymore. I had been to that place in my life that I could never return to, and the booze had indeed been a big part of it.

A few weeks later Lena was contacted by her family in Calgary. A very special aunt was extremely sick, and needed someone to look after her while she tried to recover. The caring girl I had grown very fond of never hesitated. She explained that there was a closeness between her and this woman; and no matter what the outcome was, she wanted to spend some time doing what she could to help. I told her she should go; sometimes when you hesitate, you have to live with guilt down the road.

Not wanting Art and Lydia to be left high and dry, she asked her sisters, Teena and Olga, to come take her place in Stettler. They readily agreed.

Anticipating her absence, I suddenly realized how much her friendship and company meant to me. The night before her departure, we took a walk down to the park. As we strolled leisurely along the shadowed pathway, her hand found mine.

Slowing down, we stopped at a bench. I took her in my arms and kissed her, long and gentle. When she finally pulled away and looked into my eyes, I didn't know what to expect. She kissed me back, with a lot more intensity. Breathing heavily now, she explained to me that she had never been with a man before and felt awkward and self-conscious.

"Alex," she said, "I'm feeling a lot of things at this moment and am not sure..."

Interrupting her, I softly spoke. "Lena, it's okay, just relax. Don't think too much. Let me hold you for now...we don't need to rush this. I want you desperately, but I don't want to lose my best friend. Once we cross that line, there's no going back. How about we keep walking and then head home for coffee?"

I can't believe I'm saying this, I thought.

"Thank you," she said. "You are mine, too."

Confused, I asked, "Are what?"

"You are my best friend too." With that, she leaned her head on my shoulder, and we slowly walked back to the hotel.

Her train left the next morning at 8:00 a.m. Lydia and her sisters were all there to bid her bon voyage. Art and I stood back until the hugs and tears were over. Then, as the conductor hollered "ALL ABOARD," Lena came to me and wrapped her arms around me in a warm embrace. Looking up through teary eyes, she said, "Wait for me, soldier boy; I'm coming back." We kissed passionately.

Again the conductor bellowed his impatient command. With that, she turned and quickly climbed the steps. The iron horse belched black smoke and puffed out steam. The wheels spun, then grabbed hold and headed down the track.

Everyone hollered and waved their goodbyes. I too waved, but the lump in my throat didn't allow my vocal chords to function. We stood there and watched the train chug away into the distance. I felt Lena's family staring at me. Lydia broke the silence with a loud "Harrumph!" Smiles and giggles emitted from the sisters.

Olga laughed and said teasingly, "Come on, soldier boy. Let's all get back to work now!"

Art exclaimed, "Okay, girls! Leave Alex alone." He turned his head and gave me a wink.

Chapter Seventeen

THE FOLLOWING COUPLE of weeks at the bar were good. I missed Lena but was able to keep busy. I enjoyed having a purpose and knowing that my work was appreciated. Art was always giving me a pat on the back and encouraging me. The chairs and tables were repaired and varnished. The walls were a sparkling knotty-pine clean. The big old chandelier actually worked now and looked really great all lit up. In the back of my mind, I felt that this was something that would please Lena when she got back.

I waited for her letters and enjoyed reading them over and over. Her aunt, unfortunately, wasn't doing well and Lena was unable to say when she would be returning. My replies were always filled with the message that she should take all the time she needed. In my mind, though, I wanted her to hurry back.

The long summer days had left us, and in the evenings there was a definite chill in the air. I had developed friendships

with a few of the regulars and enjoyed a newfound camaraderie with the ranchers and farmers. All salt-of-the-earth,
hard-working, decent Albertans. So far, none had given
me any trouble to speak of at the bar. Sure, there were
some fights and squabbles when the boys let off steam, but
nothing Art and I couldn't handle. Basically a quiet little
prairie town.

That is, until a bunch of hard cases showed up on a Friday
night already liquored up and looking for trouble.

They came in hooting and hollering and demanding
service. The ringleader was a puffy-faced man with a big
red nose and small beady eyes. He took a table by the door,
the others pulled chairs together around him.

I walked over and asked them what they wanted to drink.
The fellow with the pig face replied, "Beer, cold and wet
for me and my boys, and draw one for yourself!"

"Coming right up, gentlemen. Anything else?" I asked.

One of the bunch, a scruffy man with foul-smelling breath
and greasy hair, laughed. "'Gentlemen'? 'Gentlemen'? This
fool thinks we're gentlemen!"

"Shut up, Rafe!" Pig-face hollered. "You're sure not a
gentleman! In fact, you stink up the place! Now let the
waiter be; he's trying to be nice!" The rest just laughed.

"Sorry about that, mister; my friend here is uncouth. My
name is Big Jim! What's your handle?" he slobbered.

"Name's Alex," I calmly replied.

"Alex what?" Pig-face wanted to know.

"Alex Bonenfant," I said.

"Alex what...?" he asked.

"Bonenfant," I quietly repeated.

"What the hell kind of name is that?" Pig-face went on.

"Canadian, French Canadian," now with an edge to my voice.

"You hear that, Jim? He's one of those Eastern Frenchies, a real live pea-souper!" Rafe said.

"Shut up, Rafe!" Big Jim bellowed again.

I slowly backed away and went to the bar for their beers. "Trouble coming, Art, watch yourself," I cautioned.

"Don't worry, Alex, I got old Betsey here ready and waiting!" He patted the sawed-off shotgun under the bar.

"Hopefully we won't need that; just keep everyone else away," I said calmly.

Frank Stone, one of the new regulars (who had taken a liking to Olga), offered his help.

I responded, "Thanks, Frank, let me and Art handle this." Walking back to the tables with the trays of beer, I started doling them out in front of each man. "Here you go, boys, two for each of you, Stettler's best suds. That will be four bucks, gents; who's paying?"

"Here's your money, Frenchie. Hey, this ain't right," Big Jim bellowed. "I told you to draw one for yourself!"

"Well, that's real kind of you, Jim, but I don't drink anymore," I said. "Thanks anyhow."

"Don't drink? What kind of man are you? Rafe, Frenchie here don't want to drink with us!"

"Told you, Jim, them 'frogs' is odd!"

My eyes on all four hard cases now, I watched Big Jim pull a very large knife from his belt. "See this, Frenchie? Got this from my Pappy. Brought it up all the way from Texas. His uncle died and left it to him, and he gave it to me. They call it a bowie knife, and this one has gutted quite a few hombres, I'm told." He smiled as he fondled it, his piggy eyes glazing over, then suddenly stuck it into the centre of the table.

The bar went silent, except for the sounds of chairs scraping as customers moved back out of the way.

"Jim, calm down!" said one of the other men at the table. "Don't mess with this guy! I know him from somewhere! How the hell do I know you, mister?"

"Shut up, Mac! I'll handle this!" Big Jim said.

A big smile of recognition now swept across my face. "Well now, Mac...it's really good to see you again," I said politely. "You made it back alive, eh?"

"JIM, DON'T!" Mac shouted.

Too late. Big Jim made the mistake of standing up and reaching for the bowie in the table. Grabbing his outstretched hand, it was easy to twist, lift, and turn his arm just as Mac stood up, knife now in hand. The side of Mac's face turned crimson as his ear was deftly severed by the razor-sharp blade his brother held. Blood spurted everywhere as Mac hollered in pain. The knife clattered away into the corner.

Incensed now, Jim came at me with balled fists. "I'll kill you!" he screamed.

Crouching on one leg, I kicked hard at his straight knee; his bones crunched loudly.

He dropped. Immediately, I smashed his head into the table as he slid to the floor, his face now a bloody mess also.

Turning to the other two deadbeats, I quietly asked, "Who's next?" Rafe suddenly sobered up and pleaded not to be hurt. The other hard case put up his hands and vigorously shook his head. "Get these animals back to their cages and don't ever show your face at the Royal Hotel again," I said.

As the two able-bodied men carried and dragged their friends to the door, I noticed the bowie knife in the corner. Deftly picking it up, I hollered to Rafe, "Here, you forgot this!" The knife flew through the air and stuck in the wooden door just inches from Rafe's nose. He struggled to pull the knife out and then they were gone.

Art was at my side now, holding the sawed-off shotgun. "You okay, Alex?" he asked nervously.

"I'm sorry, Art, I didn't want to bring trouble to your place, but I had an old Army score to settle with the one called Mac. It's a long story, and I'll fill you in on it someday."

Frank was right behind Art. Also visibly shaken, he said, "That was incredible; if I hadn't seen it with my own eyes, I wouldn't have believed it! What sort of job did you say you had in the Army, Alex?"

"Just another soldier, Frank," I replied. "Well, let me clean this mess up, boys." I reached for the mop by the closet.

"Okay, everyone, show's over. I'm buying everyone a round on the house!" hollered Art.

"That's pretty special," Frank remarked loudly. "Anyone ever recall Art doing that before?" The bar broke into laughter and cheers.

After things returned to normal, Frank took Art off to the side. "I've heard of that bunch, Art; they're all bad news and are not going to forget easily. There's four boys and the old

man; they have a small spread up by Bashaw. Nasty people...
Maybe give Alex the heads up, eh? This isn't over yet."

"Thanks, Frank, will do!" Art replied.

Chapter Eighteen

THE NEXT DAY started out great. Lydia picked up the mail and brought me the usual letter from Lena. Stuffing it into my pocket, I wandered out behind the hotel, found a quiet spot on a bench, sat down, and began to read. The news virtually jumped out at me: Lena was coming home in a few days! The elderly aunt had recovered sufficiently and ordered her back to the family in Stettler. She was extremely grateful for all her help but wanted Lena to get on with her young life.

I smiled in anticipation.

Lydia came out of the hotel and sat down as I re-read the letter. Her smile met mine. "You got the same news in your letter, didn't you?" she asked.

"Yup!" I said, grinning now from ear to ear.

Lydia didn't say a word, just quietly reached over and gently patted my arm. She sighed, got up, and started back inside. Then, turning around, she faced me again. "This is something special, Alex. Don't you dare hurt her. We all care so much for her—not just me, but all my family. You, being quite a bit older, have worldly savvy; she doesn't. She still believes everyone is honest and sincere."

Looking straight at the eldest sister, I slowly and quietly replied, "Lydia...she's all I've been thinking about since that train pulled away from town. She's everything to me. She pulled me back from the brink. She's my best friend; I would do anything for her, and I want her in my life."

Lydia looked deep into my eyes, then replied, "Good, that's what I wanted to hear. You're okay, Alex Bonenfant." With that, she went inside.

The sun was about to set on the cool, beautiful autumn day. The train began to appear way off in the distance. Its whistle blew long and loud and black smoke signalled its approach. Again all the family and myself waited patiently on the train platform, save for Art, who had graciously allowed me the evening off. He and Frank Stone were looking after the Royal Hotel for the moment.

The noisy, smelly, iron beast finally came to a stop. A portable wooden step was put in place. Lena was the first to get off. Her sisters made such a ruckus you would have thought the Queen herself was about to disembark. I stood back and waited. Finally, the hugs, kisses, and chatter subsided, and her gaze looked over her sisters' heads and locked onto mine.

Stepping forward, she almost leapt into my arms. "So, are you glad to see me, or what!" She laughed saucily. We held each other and kissed passionately. Still holding on to each other, we blurted out at the same time how much we had missed each other. Everyone began laughing at the happy reunion scene.

Lydia finally said, "Well, Alex, don't just stand there; grab her bags and let's head over to the café. Coffee and cake are waiting!"

The noisy gathering was slowing down; Teena and Olga had already left, and Lena announced how tired she was from the long train ride back from Calgary. She was tuckered out and was going to turn in. I caught the wink in her eye and said that I should head over to the bar and make sure Art and Frank were okay.

That was precisely what I did. They were fine; it was a quiet night, and they really didn't need me. "Okay, gentlemen, I'm going to call it a day; see you tomorrow!" I said. With that, I was out the door and headed to my comfortable little shed. Anticipating possible company, I had spent considerable time cleaning and making sure everything was as neat as it could be.

An hour had passed, and I was beginning to think maybe I had read her signals wrong. Then, there it was, a quiet tap on the door, a giggle, and she was inside. The coal oil lamp was turned down low, but even in the soft light, her eyes sparkled like heavenly stars.

Our embrace was instantaneous. The passion in our kiss was delirious. Weeks of waiting were now over; we gave ourselves to each other. Finally pulling back, Lena breathlessly said, "Alex, no matter what happens in the next few moments, this is where I want to be. My mother-hen sister, Lydia, says that you are older and too experienced in the ways of the world and that I should be careful. I don't care. I just know that you are the man I want."

"Lena, all I could think about while you were gone was how much I missed you. Your sweet innocence, beautiful smile, and wisdom, my dear friend, is genuine. I'm afraid I have fallen hard for you," I sincerely replied.

"Hold me, Alex. I don't ever want you to let me go."

"Lena, this moment has to be special; let's not rush. I want you to know how wonderful intimate love can feel." My heart pounded in my chest. In the shadow of the lamp, I watched as she slipped off her jacket, then her dress, and soon was completely naked in front of me.

Reaching for me, she said, "Well, are you just going to leave your clothes on?"

"Not a chance!" I said, as they fairly flew off. I gently laid her on the bed and slid in beside her as I caressed and kissed every part of her body.

The sensuous moments of the rest of the night were almost magical. Finally, exhausted and sublimely satisfied, we lay in each other's arms.

"Alex...I had no idea it could be this good..." Lena quietly said. "Is it like this all the time?"

"It's always great when you are with someone you care deeply about," I replied, the afterglow and tranquillity of the moment causing me to sleepily drift off.

"You're not going to sleep now, are you?"

"No, of course not," I lied. "Just resting my eyes and enjoying what we have."

"That was so nice; can we do it some more?" she asked.

"Of course, sweetheart. Anything you desire."

"Good, only this time I want to ride on top," she giggled.

"You're insatiable, you rascal!"

"That's a good thing, isn't it, Alex?"

"Yes, Lena, that's a damn good thing!"

All too soon we could see the early hue of dawn starting to come through the curtains.

Lena reached for her clothes and quickly dressed. "I need to get back into my room in case Lydia decides to check up on me. You know she's an early riser," she said.

"Maybe we'll get lucky, and Art will be entertaining her this morning," I quipped.

"Maybe," she laughed. "Our family seems to enjoy the finer things in life." With that, she gave me a peck on the cheek and was out the door.

A broad smile spread across my face as I lay back on the pillow and closed my eyes. "Yup, Stettler sure seems more and more like home."

The next week was a wonderful routine of working around the hotel, building and fixing whatever was in need of repair. Lydia wanted the storage room attached to the bar enlarged and refurbished. As this was a larger project, Art hired Frank Stone to give us a hand. He was always hanging around Olga anyhow, so Art figured he might as well put Frank to work.

My evenings, of course, were spent enjoying Lena's company. Life was sweet...so very sweet! You know sometimes how everyone says that when things are going good, that's the time to watch out? Well, welcome to my world!

Frank and I had just finished the last of the general framing on the larger room when Lydia came into the bar area. She looked like someone was about to be hung. That someone, as it turned out, was me.

"Alex," she fairly snarled at me, "there's someone wanting to see you over in the coffee shop!"

"Okay..." I slowly replied, "did they say who they were?"

"Yes! The lady says she is looking for her husband...a Mister Paul Bonenfant!"

"What the hell?!" I said.

I quickly strode into the Royal Hotel coffee shop from the side door entrance. I spotted her right away, sitting with her back to me as she looked out the window. No mistaking those blonde curls; even from behind, I knew who that was.

There was Beatrice! Still a beautiful woman, with elegant clothes, looking good. Behind the counter, at the back, I could see Lena, her hands wringing a dish towel, watching at a distance, worry evident on her face. Lydia now stood protectively with her arm around her younger sister's shoulders.

"Bea, what on earth are you doing here?" I asked.

She turned quickly, a bit startled by my sudden presence. "Hello, Paul...you look good," she quietly replied. "Can we talk?" Her red eyes met my angry gaze.

"There is nothing I want to say to you, Bea. Nothing!"

"Please sit; there's much you need to hear." I looked out the window and spotted the very fine automobile she had arrived in. Two very large and efficient-looking military types were waiting outside.

My fists clenched and I felt the vein in my forehead pulsing. "Sure, why not? Joey? Is he here?" I asked, half expecting a bullet to be sent my way.

Looking directly at me, she said, "That's one of the things I came here to tell you, Paul. Your brother Joe is dead." The tears flowed freely down her cheeks. "Oh Paul, I wish I could make up for all the wrong that has happened to you!" she sobbed. "I had no idea you were still alive, even up to a couple of months ago. Joey had found out he was very ill and did not have long to live," she went on.

"His dying wish was to come back to Canada, find you, and beg for your forgiveness. He made it as far as Calgary, and that is where his life ended. He made me swear I would find you and come clean with all that had gone on at the end of the war. He sincerely loved you and needed you to know how sorry he was." Her head drooped as she cried.

I sat there looking at her, not saying a word, trying to comprehend what she had just said. Finally, I found my voice. I said, "The two of you took my life, my family, and all the reasons to keep on going. You robbed me of my identity, tried to have me killed, and almost destroyed my sanity. Forgiveness? But here's the shocker, Bea; do you know what kept me alive all that time in prison?"

She just shook her head.

I quietly said, "It was my hatred for the both of you. Now, gratefully, that hatred has passed. Now...I just feel pity."

Both of us sat there looking at each other, saying nothing; we didn't need to.

Everything was gone, a lifetime I had been working hard at trying to forget. Words couldn't change anything.

Finally, Bea uttered an almost inaudible "I'm truly sorry, Paul; it could have been so different... we had it all, didn't we? Now I feel so empty and alone. Maybe, if you could find it in your heart to forgive me..."

I stood up and said, "Bea, it's time for you to leave; there's nothing for you here in Canada."

"Have you forgotten about your daughter, Samantha?" Bea quietly asked.

"Of course not," I replied. "There isn't a day goes by where I don't think about her. With no possible way to contact her, I pray her life is going well. Is she okay? What have you told her about me?" I asked.

Taking a deep breath, she replied, "She thinks her daddy was always Joey. He had the official birth records altered to make it look that way. I didn't want him to do it, but he felt it would be best for her. Less complications." Her lip trembled.

"You two really thought of everything, didn't you?" I said, the anger starting to build up again in my body. "He even stole my own daughter from me! I never had any real time to get to know her. Hard to believe...my own brother..."

"Paul, you don't have to worry; she is fine and will be raised in the best schools in England. She will want for nothing. Joey was an extremely wealthy man with friends and influence in very high places," Bea went on to say.

"Thank you for that, Bea; I appreciate that. I know that even with all the trouble we have both been through, you would still look after best interests. As long as she is properly taken care of, that's all I want. Maybe it's best to just leave things the way they are. I never did find out how Joey became so powerful and well-connected. The tentacles of that society reach all over the world, don't they?" I asked.

"Paul, you have no idea, and it's something that you should not pursue. All of our lives would be in jeopardy."

"Don't worry, Bea, I have no plan to. I want nothing to do with any of you people ever again."

With that, she also stood up, looked out the window, and sighed. Her two bodyguards and fancy car awaited. "Goodbye, Paul. I hope the rest of your life turns out much better. If you ever get back to England, come see me," she said.

"That will NEVER happen, Bea; my home is here. There are people here who genuinely care about me—honest, sincere people. By the way, the name is Alex."

Bea turned toward the door, slowly walked past, and on the way out nodded to the two women behind the counter. I watched as she got into the car. One of the bodyguards dutifully held the door for her. Then she was gone, the dust rising up as they left. I was suddenly aware of how quiet it had become.

Then a gentle hand grasped mine, and a sweet, friendly voice asked, "Alex, are you okay?"

As we stood on that wooden sidewalk holding hands, I replied, "Yes, Lena, I'm fine. Let's go get that coffee. I have a lot of things to talk to you about."

Lydia suddenly appeared at her sister's side. "Is everything okay here, Lena?" she asked quietly.

Looking up at me now, Lena replied, "I don't know...is it, Alex?"

"Lena, you are everything I could possibly want in a woman. Please don't feel threatened in any way. A part of my past has just manifested itself. I'm sorry you had to find out about Bea this way. To tell the truth, I'm pretty shaken up about this whole revelation myself. Lydia, would you be so kind as to tell Art I might be a while getting back to the bar? Lena and I need some time alone right now."

"Don't worry, you two, take all the time you need. I'll talk to Art."

We slowly walked up to her room. Sitting down on the bed, I held her hands and looked into her young innocent eyes. Then I patiently tried to make Lena understand the absolute need for secrecy, for the safety of everyone involved. She nervously agreed.

I began. "I'm about to tell you things that can never be repeated to anyone. Do you understand? No one, ever."

"Yes," she slowly replied.

It actually felt good to let Lena in on some of the most guarded secrets of my past.

Somehow...breathing became easier. To her credit, Lena listened patiently, at times incredulously, to the condensed version of the last few years of my life. The treachery, the deceit, torment, and attempt to have me killed by my own powerful brother. Then the involvement of the military to silence and cover up things until the war was over. Even the existence of an extraordinary worldwide organization that had no borders or boundaries. As I spoke, her eyes were wide; at times she shook her head in disbelief.

When I stopped, the silence of the room was deafening.

She softly spoke. "Alex, I am so sorry."

"Why on earth would you be sorry?" I asked.

"Sorry that you had to endure all those terrible things," she replied.

Slowly I realized that her hands were trembling. "It's okay, sweetheart; it's time I faced all those demons head on, and I'll survive. I can't change my past, but it's over now, gone. What I am looking at now is the future: our future, if you'll have me?"

Her eyes misted over as she looked up at me. "Alex, of course I'll have you. I have never met anyone as decent and honest. Your courage, compassion, strength, and integrity are what I admire and love most."

After a brief moment, I replied, "Did you just say love, Lena...?"

"Yes, you big lunkhead, I did; I love you!"

Smiling now, I replied, "I am no longer just smitten, girl, I am head over heels in love with you too."

Chapter Nineteen

I SPENT THE NEXT few days trying to get back into the routine of looking after the hotel. Somehow I had been allowed back into Lydia's good graces. I suspected Lena had talked to her and convinced her I wasn't some lecherous opportunist. Frank and I had finished the addition to the supply room, and it looked great. Things were good again.

As always, that was when I should have started to be on the lookout. I don't know why, but trouble just seemed to have a knack for finding me.

It was late Friday afternoon; Art and I were getting ready for the locals to start showing up at the bar. Nothing seemed out of the ordinary, but I had an uneasy feeling.

Suddenly Frank burst through the side doors. He had just come from the livery stable down the street. His friend, who ran the place, had told him to get back to the hotel and warn Art and myself. A group of real hard cases from up around Camrose had just left. They had been drinking out back and were bound for the Royal Hotel. He said he had heard them talking about how they were going to teach Art and me a lesson in manners. One was hobbling on a crutch, and another had a missing ear.

As this news sunk in, Art reached behind the bar to make sure "Betsy" was loaded and ready. He told Frank to tell Lydia to get the law down here as soon as possible. Trouble was coming. Frank quickly did so and returned carrying a baseball bat.

Suddenly the main doors opened wide, and an old man with a weathered, greasy cowboy hat was standing there. He squinted as he made his way in. The rest of the family followed behind. There was Jim (Pig-face), Mac and Rafe, two other brothers who looked like they were the product of some kind of unnatural coupling, and two more bad-looking characters. One of them had a telltale bulge under his coat.

As the old man reached a table, he and his crippled-up son sat down. Mac and Rafe stood off to the right, and the rest sidled to the table to the left of them.

"Good evening, Garth," I said pleasantly. "How have you been? Haven't seen you since I first got off the train here in Stettler."

Still squinting, the old fellow said, "Eh? How do I know you, mister?"

"Helped you get that heavy trunk off the train and loaded on a cart a while back. Name's Alex; you remember now?"

"Yeah, yeah, now I do."

"So what brings you to town, Garth?"

"Well, it seems someone in this bar laid a licking on two of my boys a while back. Jimbo here is crippled up bad with his knee all busted up. Mac done had his ear cut off and can't hear so good no more. My two ranch hands (he now pointed to Rafe and his partner) say it was some crazy Frenchman who went nuts all because he didn't want to drink with them. What do you know about that?" he asked slyly.

"Garth...that would be me," I replied. I noticing Mac and Rafe slowly changing their stance. "You're welcome!"

"Welcome? What the hell are you talking about?"

"I sent you your boys back alive, didn't I? Can't guarantee that's going to happen this time..."

"Eh, what did you say?"

Jim spoke up now, "Pappy, he says he might do us in this time!"

"You sure are a cocky son of a bitch, mister, I'll give you that! Can't you see you're a bit outnumbered here, boy?" Garth taunted.

"Nope, all I see is a pig-face cripple, his cowardly inbred brothers, and a couple of hired hands. I'm asking you politely to leave these premises, as these men were formerly informed that they are not welcome here."

By now Art had manoeuvered himself close enough to cut the occupants at the table in two, should the shotgun he had deftly hidden by his side be brought to bear.

"You sneaky devil!" Garth hollered.

"So, what's it going to be, Garth?"

Big Jim, incensed at the turn of events, decided to pull out the very large bowie knife and wave it around the table, pointing it at me and also in front of his father.

"Jim, you have to be the stupidest person I have ever met!" I said. "The last time you did that, you cut off your brother's ear! Who's next—your old man?"

"What are you boys waiting for? Cut him down!" Jim screeched. His two dim-witted brothers at the other table didn't move. Art had that shotgun pointed right at them. Maybe they weren't so dumb.

Garth slowly spoke. "You cut off your brother's ear, Jimbo?"

"What? It was him, Pappy; he made me do it!" Jim whined.

"You stupid bastard!" Garth hollered. "What did I do to deserve all you morons?"

"Jim, I'm going to ask you to put the knife down!" I said. "Garth, please tell your man over there I know that he has a .45 tucked in his belt. He pulls that out, and you are all going to get hurt. That shotgun of Art's has a hair trigger!"

"Well, I'll be!" Garth said hesitatingly. "Looks like you gents have the drop on us. Okay, boys, enough is enough. This fellow outfoxed us fair and square. Take that .45 of yours and put it on the floor, Ralph, and be careful; I don't want it to accidentally go off and kill one of us! Do it now!" Garth gruffly commanded.

"Okay, Boss, whatever you say." Ralph gently lay the gun down on the floor in front of him.

In the meantime, Mac had sneaked around to the front of me. I knew what he was up to but didn't want to take my eyes off of Jimbo and that small sword of a bowie knife.

"That's using your heads, fellows; I really didn't want to clean up a lot of blood and guts tonight," I said.

Frank had now managed to ease into striking distance of the one called Ralph, his bat ready.

Big Jim cursed. "No, not again, Frenchie. This time you're going down! I'm going to kill you. You asshole!" With that, he lifted his arm and let the bowie fly.

Suspecting that idiot might do something stupid, I was ready. I dove to the floor; the nasty cleaver sliced through the air close enough to nick my cheek. As I rolled, my hand grasped the "toothpick" in my ankle sheath and instinct took over.

Big Jim never saw it coming. The slim throwing knife was now embedded in his throat. His eyes were wide, and although he didn't know it yet, he was a dead man.

Pandemonium broke loose. Ralph made a grab for the .45. Before he could reach it, though, Frank swung hard with his bat. Ralph's head spurted crimson blood all over the place. The .45 clattered away harmlessly.

The two dim-witted brothers roared with anger and then lunged at Art, both reaching for some kind of weapon hidden in their jackets. Sure enough, the hair trigger on the shotgun erupted. At that range, the blast took them both out at the same time. Blood and gore spewed onto the walls and floor.

That left just the old man, Mac, Rafe, and the other hired hand. To my amazement, the bowie knife had caught Mac in the hip and he was now white as a ghost. Blood spurting out of his wound; it looked like an artery had got cut. He was obviously going into shock.

A quick thought crossed my mind. That damn bowie knife of Jim's was always cutting up Mac somehow. He was like a bloody magnet, literally.

The hired hand had his arms in the air. He wanted no more of this mess. Garth just sat in his chair, dumbfounded.

"This isn't how it was supposed to end up!" he cried, looking at his devastated family strewn around him. He began blubbering uncontrollably, watching the last moments of Jim's life with wide eyes, his body shaking spasmodically in the death throes. The two heaps of bloodied flesh blown against the wall, once his progeny, twitched and quivered.

The acrid gun smoke hung in the air along with the familiar copper smell of blood. Rafe was bent over trying to help Mac. He was hollering to pull the knife out. I reached over and grabbed Rafe's hand. I said, "Pull that pig-sticker out and Mac's going to bleed out for sure. Here's a rag; put pressure on that wound and don't let go. Wait for the sawbones to show up!" Mac's head flopped back as he fell into unconsciousness.

Some of the early-afternoon patrons were now coming out from under the upturned tables, where the smart ones had taken cover. I hollered over to Art and Frank, "You two okay?"

Both men were trying to catch their breath. Then Frank began to retch off to the side. "Yeah, we're fine, Alex. You?" Art replied

"Yup...doing a lot better than these chuckleheads!"

Just then Lydia and Lena burst through the side doors with the RCMP constable right behind them. "Holy shit!"

he exclaimed, "What the hell happened here, Art?" He had his gun out now. The constable turned to one of the patrons. "Charlie, you run down and fetch the doc, pronto!"

Lydia, crying loudly, ran to Art and wrapped her arms around him. "I knew this stupid bar was going to bring us trouble, Art! I just knew it!" she said between sobs. He was still holding the smoking shotgun, shaking like a leaf now.

Lena, also shaking uncontrollably, grabbed me close. "That's a pretty deep cut on your cheek, Alex; I'm going to have to sew that up."

The blood was now streaming down my face and neck. "I think I can wait until your hands are a bit steadier, sweetheart," I said, smiling at her. "No rush, I've had much worse." She found a clean cloth and gently wiped my gash.

The constable started to take charge. "Art, you need to put that shotgun down."

"No problem, Ken, the damn thing's empty anyhow," Art replied.

"You boys over by the tables, help move that fellow with the knife in his hip out of the gore. Don't pull that knife out, whatever you do! Frank, if you're finished puking, get over to the door and lock it up! I'm closing this place down until I get everything figured out." He quickly walked over to Garth and said, "You got any weapons I should know about? Step away from the table and put your hands where I can see them—now!"

The old man, still sitting, slowly put his head down, his hands outstretched for the lawman to see. He continued to moan, "My boys, my boys, what have I done?"

Just then the town doctor showed up with his bag. "Good God! You gents sure buggered up my evening, didn't you? Charlie, head over to my office, grab the big kit bag by my desk. I may have to take this poor guy's leg off."

Garth, realizing the sawbones was talking about his last remaining son, seemed to come out of his daze. "Doc, you do whatever you got to do; don't let my boy die! You hear me?" he hollered.

"I'll do what I can. That sure is a big knife he's got stuck in him. We have to be real careful; if I don't do this just right, he's going to bleed out. I'm going to need another pair of hands. Anyone here had any medical training?"

No one answered, so I quickly said, "I'll help as much as I can, doc; I've spent a lot of time patching up soldiers in battlefield situations. What do you need me to do?"

Lena was right there by my side. "I can help too, just walk us through it!"

"Okay, Lena, fetch me a bottle of whisky to help keep the infection down," he said. "I'm going to need many towels and a lot of light to see what I'm doing. You there, you're his friend?" He spoke directly to Rafe, still holding the unconscious Mac.

"Yes, sir, I am. He's like my brother."

"Good, I need you to hold him extremely still. If he should come to, do not let him move! Understand?"

Rafe nodded.

"Alex, I need you to grab his leg and slowly try to straighten it out. Slowly, and if I tell you to stop, you stop. Understand?"

Reaching into his bag for some scissors, he cut away the bloodied clothing, muttering to himself now and cursing the stupidity of men as he worked. "Thanks, Lena, now give me that bottle of whisky." The old doc tipped it up and took a long hard pull on the jug. "Now, slowly pour some right onto the knife blade; not too much, but let it drizzle into the wound. I need to see how bad the artery is nicked. Well, now, it looks like I may be able to stitch this up as long as that knife doesn't move. Lena, gently hold the blade while I do some sewing. Are you okay?" he asked her.

"So far so good," she replied.

"You know, I could certainly use a nurse like you from time to time. You seem quite collected and have a very steady hand. You interested?"

"Thanks, Doc, I'll surely think on it, but right now my mind's not on a new profession."

"Oh yes, of course. I am truly sorry; my timing is a bit off. We'll talk another time. Alex, give me another slug of that whiskey before I tie this off.

"Okay, Lena, I need you to gently lift the knife and slowly pull it out of the wound. We need to make sure it doesn't do any more cutting on the way out. Gently, gently...great. Now, while I have the main bleeder tied off, I need you to put a stitch into that flap of flesh. I can't let go until we are sure it's not going to leak. You still okay, Lena?"

"Yes, sir," she said, breathing heavier now and looking over at me as I held Mac's leg.

"You're doing fantastic, sweetheart. Take a slow deep breath; you can do this," I said.

Bringing her attention back to the job at hand, the doc said, "Pull the knot loosely now and then slide it down over your finger just so it's snug, not real tight. Good... Here goes, I'm letting the bleeder open. Well, I'll be...damn, that's great! And that, good people of Stettler, is how we save a man's life and leg! That should hold fine; I'll just finish up with a few more stitches..."

Smiling at Lena, he said, "You are definitely a natural; you sew a lot?" Lena nodded in reply. "I can tell. Now, on to that fellow with the cracked head. Anyone check to see if he's still breathing?"

Touching the carotid artery in his neck, the old doc just shook his head. "Nope. He's a goner. Charlie, run over and get that wagon hitched up in back of my office; time to start moving these corpses out of here. You okay with that, Constable?"

"Just hold on, Doc; I'm going to need some more time to get all these statements written up," he replied. "They can wait; they're not going anywhere, are they, Doc?"

"Okay, you're the boss, Ken." He wiped his bloody hands off with the soapy cloth Lena quickly provided. "Where did you put that whisky, girl?"

Lena had her arms around my waist now, mostly for support. She was shaking again. "Do you ever get used to it, Alex?"

"Used to what, sweetie?"

"The agony and horror of death and dying?"

I quietly looked into her innocent eyes and said, "No, you don't. In wartime you just get numb. It's in the quiet times when it usually hits you. Life is so precious, and the one thing you can never do is take it for granted. You fight like hell to survive and never give up."

Constable Ken hollered over to Frank to bring a few tablecloths to cover up the bloodied bodies. Frank was as white as a sheet now. "I think I need to sit for a while, Ken," he responded.

Looking at him, the cop agreed. "Yeah, sit down before you fall down!"

What a night this had turned out to be! Finally, the bodies were removed. The officer had taken statements from everyone at the bar. When he finished with Art, Lydia asked if she could take him upstairs and have him lie down. The trauma of what had happened was now setting in.

"Yeah, Lydia go ahead," the constable said.

The doc had Mac taken over to his office. He had him doped up with morphine and he was going to live. Garth, Rafe, and the hired hand would be spending the night in jail, pending charges.

The place was now almost empty. The rest of the locals had been told they might need to show up again to go over things tomorrow. It was just me and Lena and the constable left.

I asked him, "So, what is your consensus, Ken?"

"Well, I can't say for certain yet, but it's pretty clear that you folks were the victims here. They came after you and Art. You had warned them to leave and almost accomplished that when the one idiot son threw that knife. Then it was self-defence, as far as I can see. We'll talk some more tomorrow, Alex." With that, he went out the door.

"Lena, you go on up to bed; I know you're about done in," I said. "I'll be here a while cleaning this mess up. I don't want Art trying to do it by himself tomorrow morning. Frank and Olga have left. He's really shaken up too."

"Yes, I can't hardly stand up anymore myself, Alex."

"Here, let me get you upstairs first, then I'll come back down and do what has to be done."

She leaned on me all the way up to her room, fell down on the bed exhausted, then was out like a light. I headed back downstairs. I grabbed a bucket and mop and started the cleanup. Dried blood and gore was everywhere. *That shotgun really can cut a man in half*, I thought to myself.

The doc had removed my "toothpick" from Jim's throat and left it on the table. I slowly took it, cleaned it off in the soapy bucket, and then dried it with a cloth. This handy little weapon had saved my life so many times. Grateful it was still in my possession, I carefully put it back in the ankle sheath where it belonged.

Three hours later it was done. Dog-tired now myself, I locked up the place and headed upstairs.

Chapter Twenty

THE FOLLOWING MORNING was a sombre time indeed. Art and Lydia didn't come out of their room. Lena slept late and decided, for the first time ever, that the café would stay closed until afternoon.

I was up at the usual time and headed down to the kitchen. Soon I had coffee going and had put a closed sign on the hotel's front door. Things would just have to wait until later.

Finally, Art came down and found me cleaning up in the bar. "Alex, thanks for cleaning up and taking care of things for me. I really owe you! Do you mind if we sit and talk a while?"

"Sure thing, Art. How are you doing?" I asked.

"To be honest, Alex, not very well. I didn't sleep at all last night, and Lydia was really upset too. You know, I talked her into buying this place just after the government repealed the Prohibition laws. She wasn't keen on it. She told me it was my dream, not hers, but that she would go along with whatever I wanted. It broke my heart to see her crying like that. Alex...I killed two men last night. Two others also died in my bar. I feel very responsible and don't know how to handle this whole mess." His bloodshot eyes and dark circles showed his exhaustion.

Grabbing the hot coffeepot from the bar, I poured us both a cup. Speaking slowly and looking right at him, I said, "Art, I'm not going to lie to you and say it'll be alright. It won't. You will probably have nightmares for the rest of your days. Those faces will forever haunt you. You'll go over what happened a thousand times, over and over. The outcome will always be the same, though, my friend. They are dead. You can't change that.

"In wartime, we are trained to kill. That's what soldiers do. The justification being that they are the enemy and it is either them or us. Last night that bunch of assholes came after us. We didn't want to hurt anyone. They attacked us. Just like Constable Ken will tell you today, it was self-defence. Art, you are a hard-working, honest man and have every right to stop someone from killing you or taking what is rightfully yours. The fact you are feeling this way proves your worth and integrity as a man.

"Now, you have to heal. It might be a time to take Lydia and go somewhere for a while. Recuperate and recharge yourself. Hopefully, you'll never have to take another life."

Art didn't say anything at first, just kept looking into his coffee cup. "Thank you, Alex. I appreciate you helping me figure things out. You've been through this a few times, haven't you?" he asked.

"Yes, sad to say, quite a few; it never gets easier," I replied.

Taking a deep breath, he sighed and enquired when the constable was going to be around. I replied that I didn't know; sometime today, I supposed. "How's Lena holding up?" he asked.

"She's going to be fine, Art. I'll look after her, don't worry."

Sighing again, he said, "Think I'll head up and check on Lydia."

"Take all the time you need," I said.

Just then Frank Stone came in the side door, looking as haggard and aged as Art. "That was one hell of a scary evening, eh gents?" In an unsteady voice, he asked if the coffee was still hot.

"Yup," I replied, "still pretty fresh too. Here, let me pour that for you, Frank."

"Thanks, Alex. Art, you look like shit."

"Feel like it too, Frank. How's Olga?" he asked.

"She's a tough one, Art, just like the rest of those Mix girls; they come from tough stock. Left her in the kitchen in the café. She's going to cook something up for us all this evening. Take the pressure off Lydia and Lena, I guess. She wants to help.

"Just saw the closed sign on the door, Art. Quite a few customers hanging around and talking outside. What do you want me to tell 'em?"

"Frank, tell them we are closed for today and maybe tomorrow too. I really don't care right now!"

"You got it, Art," he replied. With that, he left. Returning right away, he sat down to finish his coffee.

"Alex, I need to say I've never seen a man as good with a knife as you. That huge bowie knife was aimed right at your head, and yet you managed to twist out of its deadly path. It all happened so quickly, like a blur. You have the instincts of a big cat! That kind of training...it's obvious you weren't just an ordinary soldier, were you?"

I let the probing enquiry pass.

"Going over it all last night in my mind, it really was incredible one of us wasn't killed. Makes a person stop and think, eh?" Frank rambled on.

"That it does, Frank. That it does. Life today tastes much sweeter, doesn't it?" I said. An awkward silence pervaded the table.

"Well, boys, I'm headed up to see Lydia, be back down in a while."

"See you later, Art," we both said.

Chapter Twenty-One

THE NEXT DAY, Constable Ken came and sat down with us and gave an update on what was transpiring. Attempted murder charges were laid against Garth and his bunch, and they were being held in jail until the judge was to come through next month. Mac was going to live, but might not be walking properly for the rest of his days.

As for us, the days passed, and slowly our lives began to return to normal. The following spring, I asked Lena if she would do me the honour of becoming my wife and she eagerly said yes.

We had a small family wedding, nothing fancy, just the entire Mix clan and a lot of local friends and ranchers.

Frank and Olga got engaged a few months later.

Art had lost his zeal for the hotel business and at the urging of his wife put the place up for sale. It took a year or so, but a buyer finally came and put in an offer and Art took it. He and Lydia bought a ranch in southern Alberta and started raising their family in the foothills.

My new bride and I decided to make a change also and soon we moved to Banff. I had heard they needed carpenters and tradesmen to work on the new Banff Springs Hotel, a magnificent structure in the heart of the Rockies. This building was a showpiece, built of the best-quality materials and workmanship. The railway wanted this hotel to last over a hundred years. The goal was to attract visitors from all over the world, and they definitely succeeded. It was great to be a part of something very special.

It was an incredible time for us. Our lives were full and good. We were very happy awaiting the birth of our first child. We did miss everyone back in southern Alberta, but in reality, it wasn't that far away, and visits and reunions were always happening.

My nightmares had, for the most part, subsided, although out of the blue my mind would sometimes go back to that horrible time. Loud noises and gunshots would usually set things off. Lena would always understand, but others probably thought I was sometimes an odd duck. I didn't care. I had my family, and that was all that mattered.

I loved hiking alone into the mountains and fishing those wonderful streams in my free time. It became a place of healing for me. The wild game was abundant and just being around nature was fantastic. Often, I thought about my good friend Jackson, back in New Brunswick, and how he would enjoy this beautiful, untamed wild land. Alas, I never saw him again.

Our baby girl arrived while I was working in Banff. Lena was the perfect mom. Both of us doted on that little darling and, unintentionally, we probably did end up spoiling her some. That was okay. She could do no wrong in our eyes.

The work did peter out eventually, and it was necessary to move on. I acquired a very good job looking after the bar at the Athabasca Hotel in Jasper. Nowhere near the elegant Banff Springs Hotel, but a great place to work. I even brought little Patty in at times and parked her right up on the bar while I looked after things. The local patrons would come in and fuss over her; some even gave her money. Eventually, Lena put an end to that. She felt it just wasn't the proper environment. She was right.

Our first son was born in Jasper, and our lives became much busier. We couldn't have been any prouder or more content. But, just as at every other time in my life, when things were going good, look out. "Nothing lasts forever," as the old saying goes, and things around the world started to spiral into ruination.

The stock market crashed. We didn't even really know what the stock market was out in Jasper, but it seemed to have a domino effect on everything. The economy started to grind to a halt in Canada. We entered the time of the Great Depression, the "Dirty '30s," as some nicknamed it.

Dust storms and crop failures raged across the prairies. We went from a hustling boom time to total despair. Entire towns became vacant and empty. People were literally walking away from their homes, farms, and ranches. With no way to feed livestock, everything that could be sold was gone. The banks were kept busy foreclosing on everyone. The entire Canadian population was searching for stability, but that was not going to happen.

Out of necessity, our little family moved to Edmonton. There we managed to acquire an older house with lots of rooms. We took in boarders, Lena did sewing and laundry for people, and I worked at whatever I could: carpentry, labour, anything. We planted a big garden. Anything to get by. These were tough times indeed, but somehow we managed.

Another World War was eventually spawned from the remains of the first one (the war that I had fought in, that was "to end all wars"). The familiar patriotic drums began to beat, and again the politicians and clergy urged everyone to participate or else.

Another evil German empire needed to be destroyed. The up-side was that it got everyone back to work.

It takes factories, unbelievable amounts of supplies, and a lot of steel to fight a war. Our economy was again headed up. What was amazing, though, was the ingenious new weapons that had been developed. Mankind could now kill so much more efficiently. Even so, the war still lasted about six years. Then after that came what was called the "Korean Conflict." Seems like there will always be war.

I am now of the opinion that wars are manifested to create wealth. Business interests, dollars, and manipulation of land assets are what drive them. Powerful men and groups use wars to generate redistributions of assets. Let's face it: when a war is declared, the first casualty is truth.

Chapter Twenty-Two

OUR KIDS WERE grown now and for the most part were involved in their own lives. We enjoyed the quieter times and had settled into a retired lifestyle. Things were good. Less stress and activity. Which suited us both just fine.

Of course, that's when things usually go south, eh?

I had been losing weight and was really tired all the time. I was waiting to hear what the local quack doctor was going to say. My tests had arrived back, and he had requested to see me. It was a long walk there, and I was grateful to finally arrive at his office and sit down. My strength just wasn't what it used to be. *I guess my age is finally catching up to me,* I thought to myself.

"Alex, I have to relate some discouraging news. The diagnosis is not good," the doctor stated. "You have a disease that we see all too much of these days. It's called leukemia, or cancer of the blood. I'm not going to tell you that everything will be alright because in all likelihood this is eventually going to be fatal. We can try a new treatment with radiation, and some exciting new drugs are being developed that seem to slow things down. There's always a chance."

I could tell right away he was bullshitting me about there being a chance.

"I want to admit you into the Colonel Mewburn Veteran's Hospital, where we have the best care available," he went on. He explained all the positive possibilities to me. After that, I really couldn't hear him anymore.

The news really surprised me. I knew I wasn't feeling well but figured that some rest and medication would pull me back into shape. "Well, I'll be damned," I said. "You're sure about this, Doc?"

"Yes, Alex. We have double-checked your lab tests, and along with the symptoms you are presenting, it's certain."

"So, any idea how much time I have?" I asked.

"With a little bit of luck, you may have three to four months," he replied.

Well, I guess I had better make it home and talk to Lena, I thought to myself. I decided to treat myself to catching the bus rather than walking back. Feeling a bit weak and having the doctor relay the news of my impending demise was exhausting in itself.

It was a beautiful autumn day, and the trees were in full colour. When the bus came to my stop, I sat down on the empty bench outside and looked all around. The sun shone on my face, and I could hear children playing across the street. All the pleasant little things that are a part of each day now seemed to somehow magnify themselves.

I've really enjoyed being alive all these years, I thought. *We never believe that it will eventually happen to us. Everyone thinks they are somehow going to live forever.*

Telling her was one of the hardest things I have ever had to do. Walking through our kitchen door, I hollered out, "Anyone home?"

Her sweet face, tousled hair and armful of washing came around the corner. "I was wondering when you were getting back," she said. "Are you hungry? What did the doctor have to say?"

Her reaction was instantaneous and pretty much expected. The washing tumbled to the floor as she managed to sit down at the kitchen table and utter a tearful "Oh no, Alex, that can't be right! They need to re-check those results! What on earth is leukemia?" Her eyes locked onto mine as she held my hands.

"My dear, wonderful 'soldier boy,' how am I supposed to live without you? You are, and have always been, my best friend," she sobbed. I could only manage a slight smile back at her and with a cracking voice replied that she hadn't called me that in a long time. We sat there and held each other. My heart felt like it had a hole in it.

Chapter Twenty-Three

LENA CALLED OUR children and gave them the disturbing news. I had to be at the Colonel Mewburn at 1:00 p.m. the next day to begin my treatments. Our son offered to take me there, as I had never owned a car and didn't drive. Lena insisted on coming.

The check-in at the hospital was routine. They had been expecting me, and my bed was ready. The whole place smelled like a typical hospital: lots of disinfectant, cleaning solutions, and urine.

Once everything was completed, I told my beautiful wife and concerned son to go on home, as I would be just fine. I actually wanted to be alone. They reluctantly said goodbye and assured me they would return tomorrow. Sitting on the edge of that bed and slowly looking up and down the long row of cots, I suddenly realized that I would probably never leave this place. Not a good feeling...

A very efficient-looking nurse approached me and introduced herself. She handed me some pills and a glass of water and told me to take them. I did. As she was leaving to return to her station (which was actually more like an observation post, with a completely unobstructed view of all the beds on the ward), a crusty old man in a wheelchair came over.

"I'll be damned! As I live and breathe, Paul Bonenfant, you old bastard!"

There's a voice from the past, I thought as I squinted to see who it was. "Scottie, you old reprobate! You look like Methuselah!" Coming closer now, I stood and grabbed his hand. "It's good to see you, old friend!" His weak handshake revealed his current state of health. "What the hell are you doing here?" I asked.

"Same as you, Paul." He grinned. "Waiting my turn to croak!" Both of us laughed heartily. "I heard someone by the name of Bonenfant was being signed in today and I thought he might be some kind of relative of my old war buddy. Says on your clipboard that the name is Alex, though. What gives?" he asked.

"It's a long story, Scottie. I've been going by the name of Alex now for many years," I replied. "Courtesy of the CEF military tribunal hierarchy."

"That have something to do with you busting the jaw of your asshole brother?"

"Yup. You got it!" I grinned back.

"We all thought they were going to hang you or put a bullet in your head then and there. Wartime? Striking a superior officer? You sure were pissed!"

"He had it coming, Scottie. I actually held back a little, could have driven his jaw into his brain if I wanted to," I said.

"I know you could, Paul. You taught us most of those hand-to-hand tricks, remember? How long they give you?" Scottie asked.

"Three to four months," I replied. "You?"

"Couple of weeks, if I'm lucky," he replied. Just then he started coughing and reached for a handkerchief. Finally, the hacking stopped, and as he pulled his hand from his mouth, I could see the handkerchief was covered with blood and phlegm. "Getting tired now," Scottie said. "Push me down the way to my cot, would you? I don't think I can wheel myself back on my own." His pallor was turning ashen.

"Sure thing, old-timer; you always were a bit of a pussy!"

"Up yours, Paul. Sure you can find the way back?" he cackled.

I managed to get him back to his cot and helped swing him onto it. "Give me a couple hours then come back down, and we'll talk some more," he wheezed.

"Sure thing, Scottie, just rest up a bit for now."

As I returned to my bed, I thought of all the missions Scottie and myself had been involved in. Incredible soldier. A good man to watch your back. Great to see him again! Amazing, that we meet up at literally the end of our lives in this place, after so many years.

I let Scottie rest up and then after a few hours wandered down to where his bed was. He had his back to me as I approached and when I came around the other side, I saw that his pillow was soiled with blood and more phlegm. I was certain he was unconscious. I must have woken him up hollering to the duty nurse for help.

He turned over, his eyes opened, and he looked right at me. He asked, "What the hell is the matter with you, Paul? You make a lot of racket for someone with a reputation for stealth!"

"Thought you were dead, old-timer, and they do need the space around here for legitimate sick people, you know!" I grinned at him, then pulled up a chair and asked the nurse who had just arrived to please get this old buzzard a new pillowcase, as he has been drooling all over this one. She gave me a stern look, replied that yes, he certainly needed some attention, and left.

"You know, Paul, you keep this up, and they're going to throw us both out of this place!" Scottie cackled.

"That's okay, Scottie, both of us have been thrown out of better places than this, eh?"

"Damn right!" he said.

Soon the nurse returned with not only a fresh pillowcase but a new pillow. "Paul, you must have some kind of pull around here," Scottie remarked.

"Only the best for my buddy." I smiled back at him. "Thank you," I replied sincerely to the nurse.

"You are very welcome, sir," she said politely.

"I detect a bit of an English accent; am I right?" I asked.

"Yes, you are. Most people think it's Aussie," she said.

"Oh, no mistaking an Aussie for an Englishwoman here," I replied. "What part?

"London is where I grew up, but I spent time all over Europe during World War Two. I trained as a doctor and had lots of time in military field hospitals. That's where I met my husband. He's a surgeon here at the University

Hospital." She smiled. "It took us a quite a few years to come here but finally the chance presented itself, and here we are. Uh oh, must go now, the red light is flashing at the station," she said as she got up and left.

Scottie had a big grin on his face. "You old dog, Paul, you even take advantage of a dying man's situation to hit on the ladies?"

"Put a sock in it, Scottie; I was just being polite," I replied. He started to laugh, and it brought on a particularly violent coughing spell. Soon the towel I had handed him was crimson red. He became ashen again and settled down to regular breathing. The sweet nurse arrived right away and hooked him up to the oxygen. As Scottie lay back and closed his eyes, she administered some kind of injection.

"There, that should calm him down for a while. How about you head back to your bed and let him rest a while, Alex?"

"Of course," I replied, suddenly feeling lightheaded and weak myself. I found myself sleeping most of the rest of the day and through the night.

When I awoke, Lena was there holding my hand with a worried look on her face.

I smiled and told her, "Everything's okay, sweetie. They gave me some pills that really seem to relax me. I'm not ready to croak just yet," I said, trying to be lighthearted.

"I really wish you wouldn't talk like that, Alex; it upsets me so much."

"I'm sorry, Lena. How are you holding up?" I asked.

"Not very well. I miss you. The kids are all concerned, Alex; even though they all have their own grown-up lives, they don't quite know how to handle things," she said. "You have always been the strong one in our family…" Sitting on that chair with her hands folded in her lap, she softly said, "I really need my best friend." The tears began to flow.

"Come here and hold me," I said. I made room for her on the bed. A little while later the kindly nurse from England poked her head through the curtain. "Oh, I'm so sorry, Alex. I didn't know you had company," she apologized. "That's quite all right," I said. "Please come in and meet my wife."

"Lena, this is our head nurse. I'm sorry, I never did get your name?" With a beautiful smile, she replied, "Everyone calls me Sam." My wife commented that she hoped that I wasn't giving her too hard a time.

Laughing, her reply was, "They all do, Lena! But that's okay; I can dish it out as well as they can. Alex, Scottie is asking for you, and I told him I would see if you were able to make it down to his area."

"Of course," I replied. "How's he doing today?"

She just shook her head and said, "His time is getting very short now. He has no family to speak of and I know you and him are close."

My wife said she had to leave but would be back tomorrow. With a heartfelt hug and kiss, she said goodbye.

"Someone told me you were acting up down here and that I should see if I could get you under control," I jokingly said to my old comrade.

"Yeah? Then they should have sent the entire troop in because you sure as hell can't do it by yourself." He laughed, but his voice sounded fatigued.

I leaned over and grabbed his hand. "How you doing, you old bastard?"

"I'm dying, Alex, same as you. It's not great..." An awkward silence ensued. "You still get nightmares?" he asked quietly.

Surprised, I replied, "How do you know about them, Scottie?"

In a hoarse voice, he said, "We all get them, Paul, at least those of us who were in combat. They never entirely go away, do they?"

"No...I still get them, old friend."

Scottie, his voice weak now, spoke haltingly, trying to catch his breath. "What we saw and did to survive should never have happened to anyone. The destruction, the carnage, the outright murder of human beings... It's all so obscene, isn't it? I could never figure out why the world had to go to war to avenge some royal duke in Europe. My soldiers and I really didn't give a shit. You know? Then everything just spiralled out of control."

"I agree with you, Scottie. It's like some evil force was taking pleasure in all the killings, and we were powerless to make it stop," I said. Again the awkward silence.

"Do you think there's something better on the other side, partner?"

"Yes, I do, Scottie, at least I sure hope so...tell you what, Scottie, when you get there, look around for me, will you? This time don't take a damn lifetime to reconnect, eh? When we do meet up, I know what I want to do. I want to take you to my favourite fishing stream up in the mountains. So many in the water you don't even have to put a line in. The fish will almost jump into your basket by themselves. When the sun shines the right way, it's like diamonds glimmering on the water. The sound of the breeze through the pines is like a wondrous orchestra. Air so fresh and clean, your lungs will feel young again."

"I like that picture, Paul, sounds just like heaven is supposed to be, eh," he said slowly. "You wouldn't bullshit a dying man, would you, Paul?"

"Scottie, we're going to see each other again, I promise you. You hear me?"

"I can't keep my eyes open anymore, Paul. Don't leave... just keep talking to me, okay?" His voice was becoming weaker, almost inaudible.

"I'm right here, Scottie. I'm not going anywhere."

"Sounds great, Paul...fishing in the mountains...I'm going to hold you to that," he whispered.

Now holding on to both of his hands, I told him, "Just rest, and let go...it's okay to let go, old friend," I said, a tear sliding down my cheek.

With a final breath, he did just that. He was gone...

The room suddenly felt so empty. I was all alone, holding onto my dead friend's hand. Time seemed like it had stopped. Words from an old song or poem that I had once read came into my head. Why, I'll never know. "Did you ever think, as the hearse rolled by, that you would be the next to die?"

That pretty nurse, Sam, was standing off to the side, watching and listening. She came and placed her hand on my shoulder. "I'm so sorry, Alex. You made it a lot easier for him to leave," she said. "You were a good friend."

"He saved my life a couple of times, you know," I said, my voice cracking a bit. "The sad thing is, Canada just lost another good soldier, and nobody cares. It's impossible for anyone to know what it was like back then unless you were there. That damn war follows us right to our graves."

"Come on, Alex, I'll help you back to your bed," she said. "Don't worry about Scottie's remains. We'll take care of everything."

She gave me some kind of pill and soon I fell asleep. Each day the weakness and fatigue got worse. I was losing weight, had no strength, and of course, I had no appetite left. I slept a lot.

Chapter Twenty-Four

MY FAMILY CAME up as much as they could, and it was great to see all of them. We managed to say our goodbyes and reconcile any old transgressions that had occurred over the years. I truly felt blessed. I loved them all dearly. I guess now I was ready...

They call it comatose, but I was still able to hear. My dear wife, Lena, forever holding my hand, stroked my head. I felt so sorry for her; this was taking a terrible toll. My son Gordon was quietly talking to the nurse, Sam. Lying there, I felt trapped in my own body. I couldn't move or communicate in any way. But I could listen in to their conversations, as they had moved me into a larger room with a few more chairs and some privacy for me and my family.

"So, I'm sure a story exists as to why your parents named you 'Sam'?" I heard my son ask. (Always flirting, that boy of mine.)

"Well, Sam is short for Samantha," she replied. "My mother named me that just because she liked the name, I guess."

"You came from London, I understand?" he pressed.

"Grew up in London, but my mother's family came from Lancashire. My father died just after the war, so I never really got to know him. Actually, he was Canadian also. That's one of the reasons why my husband and I wanted to immigrate here. We had always been told how beautiful this country was."

My weak heart was starting to beat faster now. *This can't be possible,* I thought to myself. *Did I hear that right? It must be the drugs causing me to hallucinate.*

My son then asked what her maiden name was. She replied, "'Bonnie.' Apparently, my father had the name changed for reasons I don't know of during the war. I have no idea what our original name was; no one could ever tell me that. Every time I would enquire of my mother, she would change the subject. Maybe they were spies or some such thing," she joked. "Oh dear, it seems like your father is having some breathing difficulties. I need to adjust the oxygen flow a bit. His respirations are faster now; I'm sorry, this doesn't look good."

The universe does work in mysterious ways, doesn't it, I thought to myself. No one would ever believe this if I told them. First, reconnecting with my soldier buddy Scottie when we were both on the way out and then this...meeting my very own daughter! Although no one will ever know; what a shame. But bloody incredible! Someone should write a book about this.

My wife still holding my hand, I took all of my remaining strength and willpower to give her one last little squeeze. I knew it was my turn to leave. Startled, she shouted, "Oh no!"

The darkness slowly started to envelop me as I processed my last thoughts. *Well, I've definitely been here in the blackness a few times in my life... Nothing to be afraid of, no more pain... just try to relax, let go, and see what comes next.*

Chapter Twenty-Five

M Y MOTHER HAD been talking for a couple of hours now. Except for the odd interruption and gasp of disbelief, I let her talk. We had shared tears, anger, and a closeness throughout that short time. It had been surprising and nice, like two close friends talking, not a mother and daughter. A side to my mother that I never knew.

She had confided things to me that had been bottled up inside her for a lifetime. Finally, she stopped, looked straight at me, and waited. "Do you hate me, Patty?" she asked.

"Of course not, Mom, why would you think that? Are you okay?" I asked.

"It feels so good to get all these secrets out. I gave your father my solemn promise to never speak of these things. He was always afraid for our safety," she said.

Just then Rose came by again and asked if we needed some more coffee or something to eat.

"No thanks, Rose, maybe a cup of tea?" my mother asked.

"Coming right up," she said with a smile, and then was off.

"So, I have a half-sister somewhere in England?" I asked.

"I don't know, Patty; we never heard from those people again."

"The war and the military brass really did a number on Dad, eh?"

"Yes," she replied. "And so did his brother!"

"What was this secret society that his brother belonged to, Mom?"

"I have no idea, Patty, and I don't want to know. Their power and grasp transcend all countries. I knew that those war records Ross is asking for could stir up a hornet's nest, so I had to tell you everything. We don't need trouble, Patty."

"Mom, World War One ended in 1918. This is 1975."

"I know, Patty, but I'm still afraid," she said. With that, she calmly stood up and put on her jacket. "Actually, I'm feeling kind of played out right now. I want to get some fresh air and walk home. Will you pay the bill and thank Rose for her indulgence in letting us use the back booth?"

"Of course, Mom," I said.

"Leave her a nice tip too. Okay?"

"Yes, yes," I replied. "Mother, let me drive you."

"No, thank you, dear. I need the walk; it's only a block away. You should walk more; it's good for you, and helps keep the weight off!"

"Yes, Mother, what a good idea." I rolled my eyes.

"Oh, I almost forgot; there's something in this envelope for you. I found it in some of your father's things. You can read it when you get home. Phone me later, dear."

She really does drive me crazy, I thought as I walked to the car. Not wanting to wait, I opened the envelope. There, on an old piece of paper, was my father's handwriting. It said, "A WAR CAN NEVER END UNTIL THE LAST SOLDIER IS DEAD."

I guess that war is now finally over.

CPSIA information can be obtained
at www.ICGtesting.com
Printed in the USA
LVOW11*1143290617
539580LV00005B/15/P